MRS CAPTAIN

Bhagyashri Daryani

<u>*Dedication*</u>

For my maa
Rita daryani

Author

My name is **Bhagyashri Daryani** and I am 30 years old. I am a Lawyer by profession. I have done B.L.S.L.L.B. from Rizvi Law College, Mumbai. I did my schooling from Sophia, Ajmer and M.P.S, Ajmer.

I am married and I have a 5 year old son, so I juggle between my family, child, job and my passion for writing. I sometimes do modelling and open Mic as well. I am a blogger and influencer as well, I am into content creation and video creating on Instagram and YouTube. I also make videos in my mother tongue which is **Sindhi** to promote it to our new generation and revive the culture of speaking our language. I currently live in Ajmer.

I am an outgoing person; I like to meet new people and travel to diverse places to learn about them and write stories which people have never heard before. I have zeal for writing scripts, plays, poems and even stand up comedy, being a female; I look more deeply into the emotional aspects of feminism and day to day life.

This is my second novel.

My first novel, **THE LOST 3 DAYS OF MY LIFE** was published in January, 2019. It was also a work of fiction and an element of love and life. I have a huge fan base on Instagram with more than 18k followers and people already keen on reading my second novel.

I am a fun loving and social person. My hobbies are belly dancing, hula hooping and mostly spending time with my little baby.

You can connect with me through my Instagram handle **@authorbhagyashri**

PROLOGUE

"2:05 am"

"Sorry?"

"2:05 am"

"Can you hear me? Are you okay?"

"I got a call at 2:05 am saying my husband is here."

I was repeating my sentences in half circles and looking at the rust old blue watch on the corner of the wall spoiled by the cob webs.

"Yes, I understand, can you please have a seat," a nurse in mid-fifties was touching my shoulders; I dint like it.

"Where is my husband, I got a call at 2:05 am and I have rushed as fast as I could, my daughter is asleep at home, where the fuck is my husband," I clenched my teeth in anger and spewed every word at her.

"I really don't know you are talking about whom because we have a number of casualties right now and I am afraid I can't address your grievance at the moment but can you please calm down and sit," she was trying to soothe me but I was getting all the more agitated.

"My husband, Captain Nicholas Martin, he was brought here a few hours back, I got a call at 2:05 am and I had to call my mom to look after my sleeping daughter and I hurriedly drove here in my pyjamas and see I have fallen down on your stupid stairs, why can't you put a 'caution' sign; I have bruised my knee," I pointed towards my right knee which was now bleeding. "And all you can tell me is that you don't know where my husband is." I don't know what got into me, I wasn't rude like this but I was so fearful at that moment and bitter with this irresponsible attitude of the government hospital staff that I could have bit anyone who would have argued with me.

"Please sit down, let me call the doctor in charge, here drink this."

"Can you please check on my husband if he's fine," I sat down on a squeaky wooden bench.

"Yes I will check," she reassured and left me and my dad on the bench.

I don't know what was in the paper cup, water or something else because my hands were trembling and the liquid splashed on my knees stinging the bruise I got and with that I went blank....

CHAPTER 1

Nick and I were friends since high school when he first shifted to Goa. Nicholas Martin and his widowed dad shifted in the house right opposite to ours. For years that house had been empty; so it was unimaginably dusty and filthy with ceilings coming down from places, lights hanging out, fungi on every corner, mosses all over the place, window panes broken and the front gate half closed and half lying down. So it was inhabitable, they might have got a cheap deal on it because there were rumours in our society, St. Luther's church society; that the house was haunted so is every house where no one has lived in past 10 years. Except us, everyone was catholic in this society. We were given this house by the Indian government because my dad, had worked for the Indian Police Service and while serving his duty time here in Goa, he was a part of the team trying to bust a gang who had illegally migrated here with drugs and other weapons and there was an accident where a bomb went off and people were severely injured including my dad. He was hospitalised and treated for spine and head injuries; though he recovered well in six months but as he had already served for more than 20 years, it was decided that he should be off from field duties and given a desk job for the anti drugs department. He happily took it saying that finally he will get time for his family and nagging wife, Punjabi wives are always nagging, and me; his 10 years old daughter, Aisha. He was not there at my birth, as my mom keeps complaining, he was not there for my play school admissions or my 5th grand birthday party which my mom alone took care of and he never went to any of my parent teachers meet. So basically he missed all those years when I was growing up chasing behind the people who were shitting their and others lives with drugs. So now when he had a comforting desk job with fixed timings and days off and holidays, my mother couldn't be happier.

She was on cloud nine when we finally shifted here thinking that now she will have the happiest time of her life which turned out only to upset her more after she saw the house we were going to live in. It was chipped just as every house in this society with muddy lanes and crooked walls. She was in a state of horror, looking at my dad with shocked eyes, "you said yes to this house, Amrinderji?"

My mom addressed my dad like this only with changes of tone in taking the name depending upon her moods, that she wants to show love or wants to pick a fight with him or just wants to nag about a thing; which was her usual tone.

"You said the house is nice, this is nice?" she dropped the bags on the outer cemented porch. "you worked hard for 20 years, gave in sweat and blood, took a bomb blast and got treated for months, never celebrated any festivals with us, gave on sleep and food and this is what you got for all you did? And you agreed to live here?" she had shown her protest.

"Had you seen the other two options they gave, this was heaven in front of them", my dad laughed. He always laughed; even about dead serious things.

"c'mon, this is not so bad; I know you can turn it into a pretty house just like you did a great job on the last one, right Aisha?" we high fived each other. We always high fived each other and grouped together against mom.

I and dad were a team, though we couldn't spend much time together; that's why I used to eagerly wait for my dad to show up, he was my hero. The lesser time he was with us, the more I wished he was with me. He had the habit of ignoring the gloomy talks; he would turn around every fight, every discussion into something funny and my mom used to hate it to the core. She did not like that dad is always making jokes and playing around in the house; never helping her or giving her the time she needed but now daddy had promised that all the time would be hers and some of course mine.

It took a great deal for my mom to make that place habitable, daddy helped in this time and I vouched to do everything they asked me to like bringing in the plants, buying groceries from the nearby store and painting the outside walls. For a 10 year old hand, I did a splendid job and painted the outside in pale aqua colour in just a week. I worked with dad in the garden, plucked weeds, seeded some flowers and kitchen garden vegetables. We all worked like a team and made that place a little heaven for ourselves. For one thing I know is home is place which you create with your own vibe; houses can be built by anyone but only your personal touch can it make your own safe abode; a place where you can fall, a place where you can heal, a place where you learn to live, laugh, love and care about your family and be true to the bond that god created for you.

Slowly that place started to look more homely, with us bringing some or the other furniture, rocking chair for my dad, kitchen appliances for mom, study table and Barbie dressing table for me. We used to go to the Sunday flea market located at Baga beach in north Goa. It was one hell of a place; I actually waited for Sundays so that we could go there. It became a routine for us; even if we did not had to buy anything, we would still go and window shop, eat some prawn curry and spend some time at the beach like any other happy family.

All little knick knacks at our home were from that flea market, spices, jams, coffee, artefacts, curios, curtains, lanterns, rugs, dream catchers. We used to buy a lot because it was cheap stuff; you should just know to bargain which my mom was expert in and I got that trait from her, thank god for her.

My daddy had assigned me to decorate my room in any way I wished. My room was upstairs with a beautiful attic and half open and half closed terrace.

Though my bed was old but the new starry pink bed sheets and duvets that we bought from the flea market made it look new and chic. I placed a jewellery hanger near the attic and a dream catcher on the window which opened on the street between mine and nick's house. We could actually see each other from the window itself. Because I was an avid reader, my library always travelled with me and got bigger and bigger in time. I was a girl with fewer clothes but more books. I used to bounce out of the house whenever book fairs were happening in Goa; buying books by weight and bringing in much more than I could ever read.

Years went by like this; I was one of the favourites in my school not only because of the good looks but because of the outgoing nature and my habit of participating in all curricular activities with zeal and bringing in medals. I was popular in my class and people hardly argued with me. My mom and dad finally had some years just for themselves, growing vegetables and loving each other.

Just when everything was settled, Nick entered in my life, though first I used to hate him because he was downy and weird, always depressed and unhappy about everything around him. He never used to look up or make an effort to talk to anyone, zooming in his own bubble and just being negative all the time.

I vaguely remember Nick was a very timid boy. He did not even ask me my name for months; though he might have heard it a thousand times from my mother's ranting.

When they shifted in that splintered house, my mother went and invited them for dinner as is the tradition here; it's more like practical than any sentimental value because they were still unloading their belongings and someone has to take care of their food until they settle down.

His father asked my dad about my school and admissions and everything because it was in the middle of the session and my dad promised to help with everything. Both of them clicked a glass of scotch and rambled about how the government promised them so much in return of their duties but they didn't get any, about the politics running in their respective departments and how they would like to change the system but one thing was in common that they both loved their country so much that issues like this didn't bother them much and both were content serving their Nation. Nick did not even look up at the dinner table forget about talking, he only ate what my mom served him in his plate.

His dad was a little arduous unlike my parents especially my mom always talking her heart out. My mom will tell you everything ranging from our ancient family history to the diseases that have been running in our blood to the kind of decoration she has planned for her daughter's wedding; even if the other person is least interested in listening. She is very cheerful and amiable. She even used to smile on the sinister things I used to do in my childhood where other mothers would have kicked balls out.

I was always creating problems, the issues were different in early years and it kept changing through out my growing years but I was a constant pain in her ass. Getting myself into troubles and sticky situations, up scaling all children tantrums and teenage demands; still my mom never complained, she was a true friend.

Even Nicholas started being close to mom, he shared things and thoughts with her, started confiding in her. His dad would not always understand what problems do teenagers face and he definitely did not know how to show care and love to him. He was a simple man though he had a big heart but he was poor in showing emotions, now you know where Nick got this trait from.

In our teen years, Nicholas was just like any other boy being hit by puberty, scrambled hairs on face, with a wheatish skin tone and curly hair, slender and flimsy but a tall frame, he was an average middle class Indian boy.

When parents move out to some other city, children have the toughest time; they have to deal with all the social incapacity. Parents don't quite get this, but for us; it's a fucking great deal to lose our friends we made over the years and to leave the friendship which we have nurtured. It's unimaginably tough to leave behind all our favourite places and start from the scratch to find new friends.

I was still adjusting to the life here owing to my nature but for him it was a strenuous affair. I guess I had that abhorrent habit of taking up projects which no one dare put their hands on. So I decided that I will be his first friend in school. We were in the same class so I took upon this challenge to make him friends with others as well and given the status of most loved and a bold girl, I would have achieved my target easily except that Nick did not wanted to socialise at all. He used to sit alone in the class even when I forced him to sit with me, he never surrendered; never uttering a single word, he was definitely living in a shell.

"Nick, Nick, can you please come out?", I used to shout like this in front of his house; every evening, begging him to leave his bubble for once and come out with us and hang out.

Some days he peeped outside of the window and shoed me away, others he didn't even bother to side his curtains.

"Nick, you moron, can't you just come out," I was raging one day.

"Aisha; just go, I have to study," his usual cranky face lurking from behind the windowpane.

"What's there to study so much nick, you are a smart one; I have seen your scores on test," I was adamant.

I started climbing the stairs to his room, "you wait there Nick, today I am gonna pull you out of your shoes and make you feel the grass." I was furious; no one has ever turned me down and that too so many times.

His room was immaculately clean with stacks of books and trophies and medals from his last school and some pictures hanging on the wall behind the bed, there was one with his mother and a group photo with his friends or classmates; I don't know.

"Nick, let's go out for once, can't you leave your house and loneliness to be a part of us like normal kids, you should at least know who your neighbours are." I tugged on his arm and tried to drag him out.

"Beat it Nick, don't be so miserable all day long."

"Ok Aisha, let's bargain." He stopped me along the street.

"What?" my eyes were big and eyebrows arched.

"I'll come with you today but you will stop forcing me to be friends with anyone in school."

"Urghh, why are you so exasperating. Fine; I won't bother you in school but you will have to come out here in the community park once in a while and you can't ignore me in the school, deal?"

"No one can ignore you Aisha," I guess he was taunting me.

Through all evening he just sat on a swing with his long legs touching the muddy puddles and head down as if it was some sort of punishment.

"What is your actual problem Nick?" I went and sat on the swing next to him while others were busy playing football. "Tell me what's wrong, why is it that you are always gloomy?" my swing was going way faster than him.

"I left my best friend back in Bombay, he was the only person in whom I confided for years and now I just feel its futile to be close to someone whom you know you are gonna leave again." His tone was low.

I laughed, "We are just sixteen nick and you are already behaving like some old prick. Stop being so sage about everything in life, you can't control any events that are going to come your way in future but for that you can't stop living in present and even if you have left him, did it end your friendship with him? no right. You will see him again someday and all the happiness will come back. Can't you make new friends here?"

"I don't believe in quantity, one true friend is enough for me."

"So let me be that 'one true friend' of yours," I mimicked his tone.

"You already are"

"Oh really, doesn't seems though" I was looking straight at him.

"Why would I come with you then," his long legs weren't made for these children swings for sure.

Now he was talking some sense. Nick was like this, being serious most of the times. In front of my illogical ramble, he would shut me up with his usual logical one liners.

"Ok, than stop pretending that you are more mature than all of us and don't you dare ignore me in school and at home also; be nice to me like a friend not just some high pitched neighbours."

"Yes, Aisha, can I go back now?"

"Yeah sure, ill also tag along"

He laughed, first time I saw him laughing sincerely, "Do you know that you are completely mad Aisha" and he gave two simultaneous nods at that; he had a habit of nodding his head whenever he was happy, some peculiar habits.

We walked all the way back just feeling the fresh evening breeze on our faces.

When I was about to enter my house, Nick coyly asked, "Do you want to study together Aisha".

I was stunned, "quite an achievement home boy," and I patted his shoulder twice with a proud feeling.

We went to his room and basically he studied where all I did was look around his room, his stuff, found some old pictures, questioned and irritated him about those, he answered some, chose to keep quite on others; I did not prod much and when my mom started shouting from our house that where the hell am I, only then I wished him goodnight, "see you tomorrow Nicholas Martin."

"You too Aisha Singh" and he smiled the second time for the evening; overwhelming progress made by me.

Next day wasn't much different from others, Nick sitting alone in one corner and avoiding every eye contact, though he ate with me in lunch break but did not utter a word.

Our classmates knew about us being neighbours by that time and whenever they saw us eating together; the usual stupid school rumours started, we did not bother about them much.

Every day he made substantial progress, occasional smiles, sharing his important notes with me, eating from my Tiffin, he loved the food my mom made because his dad could only come up with different breads. I used to get extra for him and that's why the school started calling us honeybee couple; it annoyed me more than him. For him only I mattered, I was the only one with whom he spoke in school so whatever others said did not even pass him. Girls would keep talking about how he only was interested in talking to me and he did not even look at other girls, guys would not like that he never became a part of any of their group activities; though he played most of the sports but that was that.

In no time, it was 10th boards; people did not have time to look out of their textbooks. Nick and I had the usual routine of studying at his house, he studied; I tried most of the times. It was hard for me to focus; my thoughts always had the most random things one could even think.

He always brought me back from the dream world to reality, I hated him for this but then he was the only one who could do that. I did not come to know but he was slowly becoming a habit and habits are scary, it's hard to make or break them. Not a single day passed without us seeing each other even if it was for a minute of chit chat across our windows.

"What do you want to become, like what do you aspire?" he suddenly asked me one day while we were solving some papers at his house.

I slammed my notebook on the easy chair that I was sitting, "as it is I am having hard time solving this and now you want to discuss about future goals, like really Nick?"

"I am not asking specifically about your future goals but you might have something on your mind that you want to do right?" he eyed me and then to his book.

"Umm, I don't know, haven't exactly figured out what I want to become though mom dad have asked me one thousand times and every time

I have told them to give me some time to think about it, sometimes I want to become an interior designer, sometimes a fashion designer, other times I feel like I should pursue journalism and appear on TV but most of the times I think of taking up literature and becoming an author; writing books and stories which people will love to tell and read. But where is this coming from right now?" I got up and went to look at his notes thinking what made him ask me all this but his notes were like some secret agent's codes which only he could decode, his handwriting was really bad.

"Okay your turn now; you tell me?" I went back to my easy chair.

"I am going to join the army." His expressions were firm and stillness in his voice, nothing less, nothing more, "The Indian Army'.

"Wow, you are sorted."

"How are you so sure about it?" I was amazed at that strong response of his, he is never so enthusiastic about anything but this time he was different, and something about his demeanour was so fascinating as if he has decided this ages ago. There was a spark in his eyes when he said "Indian Army' like he was born to be in the Army.

"Why Army?" my curiosity was high.

"It was my mother's last wish"

"When she was ill to the point she couldn't get up from the bed, she used to call me and tell stories about his father serving the Nation and my dad being in the army and telling me how she wanted to live for some more years to see me wearing my country's uniform.

I could sense the air in the room getting heavy and I knew, had this conversation continued; Nick would have cried and I have never seen a boy crying in front of me so I don't even know how to console one. Like what to do when a guy has a breakdown, and I am sure a lot of guys have breakdowns but we are never taught how to handle such situations. This is the problem of gender biased societies, we don't consider a man sobbing a good thing, we attach a taboo to the men who are emotional, who cry, who become nervous and shy, who breakdown over the issues of their personal and professional lives. Men are supposed to hide and gulp all the pain inside; why, I ask, just why? Where is this written that men always have to be strong, that they have to be calm and composed and stay tough to the face of this earth, why can't frailty be one of their sides? Nevertheless I thought it was best to avert the direction of the conversation.

"That's amazing, at least you know what you want to do with your life, I am not sure if I'll ever figure out what I want to be," I sighed.

"You will come to know eventually, one day it will all set on you; the purpose of your life."

"Purpose," I exclaimed. "Too deep for now, we are just prepping for the boards, aren't we?"

"Nothing is deep when you find the purpose of your life Aisha, instead of going astray, all your actions and thoughts will lead you to your purpose," something about him was so intriguing.

"You will see through it one day Aisha and that day will change the way you look at life."

"okay, I get it Mr purpose but right now I am only looking forward to clear these exams and will you help me out please Mr topper," I was grinning just to make him smile. I didn't know this then but his moods invariably affected me as well.

"No one can help you Aisha, where you should study text books; I always see you holding a new novel, do you even open the text books?" his gaze sharpening on me.

"Okay okay I am reading no more fiction until the boards get over, alright, happy?"

"Great, now let's get back to our syllabus, that's enough of chatting for the day."

My dad specially took a day off on our first day of exam to drop us both at our exam centre.

"How are you going to spend your holidays," dad asked while driving.

"Dad today is our first exam, why are you asking about holidays right now?" I was in a foul mood since morning because I didn't sleep a second; my syllabus was still incomplete.

Both dad and Nick knew how much I hated exams, they both laughed in unison.

"I have decided to join the gym in the morning hours, swimming in afternoon and evenings; I am going to prepare for NDA," he proudly elaborated to my dad.

"I have never seen such a young boy being so enthusiastic about joining the Army that he will start preparing right after 10th, its great Nicholas that you want to give NDA exam, your father must be so proud of you" I knew the last line was directed at me and with their little conversation going on, I was getting more irritated because I was busy mugging from the notes I borrowed from him at midnight; shouting all the way from my window; we didn't have personal cellphones back then.

"urghh… can you both be silent for a while" I was treading on the edge of my mood, "can we continue this later dad, when you come to pick us up" and my nose was back in the book.

"Okay sure sweetie" dad was grinning again.

We reached just before time. "All the best my children, do well and I'll treat you to ice-cream later," and he drove off.

"Nick all the best," I wished him in hurry and ran off to use the washroom.

"Aisha, don't get nervous, good luck," he was shouting from behind and his voice lurking behind.

Our exam halls were different so I saw him only after the exam, "how did it go?" he asked me blankly.

"sshh.. we don't talk about it; zip it, we are not going to discuss papers now like those stupid nerdy groups, what's done is done, you can't change anything now; so let's just go and have ice cream," and I pulled him along so that no one else from the class stops me to ask about 'how did it go?'

Daddy didn't ask anything because he knew asking me such questions will blew me off instead he played his favourite Jennifer Lopez in our 'Snowy'. I used to call our car 'snowy' because for starters it was white and daddy took great care of her as if she was his second child, though it was old but it could give a run to any new car; it was so well maintained. Dad used to clean it every day, polish old parts and take her for maintenance religiously.

So we all had a fun ride in snowy all the way outside of town where just near the highway connecting Arpora and Bardez; there was an old ice cream shop owned by Chinappa, he used to sell fresh handmade coconut ice cream, only coconut ice-cream and nothing else and it was my absolute favourite, whenever I had a rough day or I was upset, mom or dad would take me for coconut ice cream.

People used to flock out of town just to have his ice-cream, he must be old enough to have witnessed the partition I guess, but he was very friendly and I have seen him since childhood and he was kind enough to pour extra in my cup.

"Vanakkam chinappa," I shouted from the window of snowy.

He taught me how to say hello in Tamil and a few other words; I was great at catching vocab and keen in learning new languages.

"Aiyoo amma vanakkam, so long, why not come?" he was smiling with most of the teeth missing by now. His English wasn't fair but I told you he was very cute.

"We were studying for exams Chinappa," he poured 3 cups and we sat down on the roadside cane chairs that he had newly put up.

Only I chatted with Chinappa and he packed some for me to take home.

All the other exams just went fine for me; I did not go to his house for the rest of the exams thinking I might be disturbing him and also to avoid the heavy discussions about my unplanned future. We used to wave each other from the window of our rooms across the street and that's it.

On the last day while returning home, dad continued the conversation we left last time, "now what have you planned Aisha because your mother will go crazy if you are not doing anything for the summers."

I was gawking out of Snowy biting my fingernails lost in some thoughts.

Nick must have sensed the tension, "don't worry uncle, I'll talk to her," and they let me wander outside.

I didn't go home straight that day, purposely I asked dad to drop me on the beach, and I wasn't ready to hear all that nagging from my mother. Our house wasn't far from the secluded end of Baga beach, it was like a 15-20 minutes walk from home, "I'll walk home dad, I need some time for myself," I waved him; Nick joined me though.

The sun was still bright and hot on our heads. It was March; so off season here and not many tourists at this time. The beach was basically empty and it quite felt nice without the hustle. We started walking towards the end of the beach particularly where there were no shacks.

We sat down on some big rugged stones from where we could see the waves crashing on the lower bed of stones.

"I know it's very difficult to decide what you want to pursue but you might have given some thought to it Aisha, haven't you?"

I was still biting my nails.

"Stop eating your fingernails Aisha, I have never seen you like this, you are behaving totally opposite to what you are."

"look I'll be honest with you Nick, I really don't want to go into any mainstream profession, I don't want to be a doctor, engineer or work in a MNC, I don't even know if I am willing to work 9-5 or day in and day out, hearing that my mother will think I have gone mad because everyone has some aspirations."

"That's great, go on."

"The only thing I love the most is reading and maybe just maybe writing. But that's not even a lucrative profession, I might not even earn a single penny in my life like this but this is what I like to do. I want to travel different places and write about them, study different languages, meet new people, study them, their cultures and tell their stories which were hidden until now." "But where is the money in this?"

Nicholas was listening to me with great attention, I don't know how much he understood but he looked at me sincerely and said "so you want to become a writer and a traveller as well."

First time someone iterated the words I couldn't accept myself over the years.

"You are not surprised hearing this Nick?" I was stunned definitely with his calm.

"Why, is there any problem being a writer, I don't think so and honestly Aisha; I knew you were going to do something like this, you aren't born for the jobs that fit some criteria or a place. You cannot be confined to anything Aisha." His palm was over my hand all this time unknowingly.

"But don't you think mom will be mad hearing this?" I was worried the most because of her.

"Oh Aisha, she is one wonderful lady, after my mother; I have found a mother in her. She loves you incredibly, she might be worried for your future but that doesn't means she will stop you from doing something that you really wish, has she ever stopped you?"

"No, not really but this is a big decision Nick, it's going to affect them as well, forget about earning; I might be living off them for I don't know how long. I have read autobiographies of so many authors and they all were flat broke for the initial years and I don't know if I am doing a good thing or if it's the right decision."

He must be conscious of my thoughts so his grip tightened on my wrist. "Aisha, money is not everything; passion is. You will earn one day maybe 10 years later but at least you will be doing what you love the most and you will have no regrets. One should never have regrets; you never know when it's the last time that you are doing anything for yourself." Now we were holding hands not entwined fingers but just holding like you do naturally and you don't even realize that this moment was giving you solace.

"But then we will be in different classes Nick, you will have to take Science Maths and I'll be in Arts and Literature section," I don't know why I uttered this in front of him with such misery and disheartened face that he almost laughed, "are you worried because of this Aish?" "Stupid."

I got all flustered and registering the fact that we have been holding hands for so long that it got sweaty, I pulled my hand back but he was still looking at me and I got embarrassed so much that I got up and turned my face from him, "let's go Nick."

We were tracing the path back home.

"And what is Aish? My name is Aisha; huh." I flipped my hair open from the hair tie.

"So, I can call you anything, Aish, Ai or just A just like you call me Nick all the time." I know he was teasing me.

"Because your name is so big and my name is already small, don't chop it more, Nicholas Martin." I was giving silly explanations where he was just trying to cheer me up. "I will Aisha Singh," and in no time we were running back home leaving all our worries behind at the beach which were being washed away by the waves by now.

I think you should love someone who will make you shine, who will push you towards your growth and not look down upon you or restrain you from doing anything. Your love should be able to strengthen you in your goals and perspective as an individual. If there is love but not mutual respect for individual choices then that relationship will crumble down sooner or later.

I blew him a kiss before opening the door.

"Mom I have to tell you something," I couldn't contain myself more.

"What is it now?" she was busy and not in a foul mood so I thought this is the best time I could divulge everything to her in a minimalistic tone not trying to catch much of her attention.

"I have decided to take up Arts and Literature." I gulped the spit in my mouth and my eyes were slightly creased in apprehension.

"Okay"

"Okay?"

"What? What did you just say, Arts and Literature?" now she had me in her full notice.

"Yeah mom, I want to study Literature and write in future; who knows your daughter could one day become a bestselling author," I winked at her and instantly regretted doing that.

"So you think becoming an author is like spreading ketchup on your bread and becoming a bestseller is like peeling peas, right?" oh Punjabi mother's, why does all your comparison is with food.

I felt like choking myself, "umm no mom, I am not saying it's going to be easy but this is what I can do best maa; I can't think of myself taking up commerce or science, I just can't do that." I always addressed her 'maa' when I wanted to get things done for an additional emotional pressure but I guess today she was in no mood of meltdown with my sweet blasphemy.

"It will be a shame that such a bright girl who could become anything, even a CEO of a company is wasting her time studying about dead people." The curry behind was now burning but fumes were coming out of my mother's anger.

"Dead people; why do you think we would be only studying dead people?"

"Name one author whose play you are going to study and they are alive?" okay now there were fumes from both; kitchen and my mom. I forgot she was from Arts background too and that she didn't pursue any career and maybe this was holding her back from letting me take the same path.

I was rehearsing the names in my head, William Shakespeare; Ernest

Hemingway; Mark Twain; Jane Austen; Charles Dickens; George Orwell; Agatha Christie; Oscar Wilde, okay everyone was dead. Sure there were more but none came to my frozen mind.

"And who are 'we' Aisha?" mothers don't lose a single chance of scolding you.

"I don't think Nick is going to join you in your fancy dream world of reading novels, is he?"

"No mom; of course not, Nick has decided to join the Army and for that he has to take up Science Maths."

"See, intelligent soul, so who are 'we' once again?"

"It's just me and Avanti" I was cross now.

"Oh so that Avanti is feeding your brains now, I'll just call her mother."

"Mom, maa please stop, she is not feeding me anything." Dad was right; I should have thought about this a lot.

"I know Avanti and you have been childhood friends and you both sit together in all classes and exams and both your names start from A and your birth month is the same but that doesn't means if she will jump in the well, you will too." Classic Indian parenting.

"I am not jumping anywhere maa, why don't you calm down and listen to me first. I have decided this on my own, no one has to do anything with my decision; haven't you seen how happy I get when you take me to book fairs or when I read a new book and summarize it for you, can't you see how happy I am with words. I just don't want to take up something else and regret later. Please maa; please understand me." I was literally begging in front of her.

This time she heard me turning off the whistles behind, "Okay let's assume that you take up Literature just like me; what next? What are you planning to do after 12th?" I wasn't ready for such faraway discussions.

"Maa we will decide that together, I won't do anything stupid but for now all I know is that I am taking up literature."

"What if you never make a profession out of it just like me?" Her voice was shaking.

Daddy was waiting for the right time to enter this heated environment, "who says you didn't do anything, what you have done is the toughest job of this world darling. You do everything for us without getting paid or leaves or any incentives or acknowledgement. If I wasn't getting these stars on my shoulders; I don't think I would have had any motivation. But you; you do everything selflessly, you are the true hero of our house." My dad hugged her.

"And who cares if she doesn't earns, what we have is for her or maybe she will earn so much that she could take us for a world tour. We are only concerned about her choices and happiness, nothing else matters to me except the smile on both your faces." Now we were doing a family hug and I was thanking dad in mute for saving the situation and the day but we couldn't save the curry though.

I went running to Nick's house to tell him about the big event we just had in our kitchen but he wasn't in his room.

"Where's he uncle?" I asked his dad, he was always glued to newspapers.

"If not in his room; might be at the terrace," he dint even look up from the news paper.

I sprinted towards the terrace and was surprised to see him holding something else except from the textbooks; he was reading the Bible.

He was so engrossed; he didn't even register me coming. "Wow Nick, you read the Bible as well." I stood up close to him on the railing.

He closed it seeing me next to him, "yes I do sometimes when I miss my mom."

"And today you are missing her?"

"I miss her always but it's her birthday today so I am reading the verses here on the terrace so that she sees I am doing everything she wanted me to."

He was looking up in the sky and I swear the clouds were moving faster than their usual speed as if his mother was blessing him from above, "Happy birthday mother."

"Happy birthday aunty."

"She used to always pray in her free time and read the Bible, every Sunday we went to the church to attend the Mass. I still get that image of her in a light blue gown with her eyes closed and only the name of Mother Mary on her lips. She wanted me to read the Bible more regularly and now I am doing it for her; I have read it so many times now; I am still trying to find out the peace my mom had while she was at it." He was still looking up maybe trying to portray her mother's picture in the sky.

"You know Aisha, whenever I have confusion about anything or when I see myself stuck in a dilemma, I would think like my mother and read this and I have got so much guidance from it. Like see this; in the chapter James 1,

Verse 5: if any of you lacks wisdom, let him ask God, who gives generously to all without reproach, and it will be given.

Verse 6: but let him ask in faith, with no doubting, for the one who doubts is like a wave of the sea that is driven and tossed by the wind."

"It says that we ask God in full faith and he will show us the path but we should follow that path without a doubt because if we doubt him, we will be tossed away like a wave in the sea. That is how I decided to join the Army Aisha, I know this is the path my mother and God wants me to follow and I shall do it without a second thought."

"Nick she would be so proud of you," I couldn't come up with anything else to ease his pain so I just patted him on the back.

"I have something to tell you."

He looked at me instantly, "what, I could hear loud noises from your kitchen, some whistles, and aunty was shouting; what happened, did you tell her?"

"Yes I told her and first she wouldn't agree, but somehow I managed to assure her but the dinner is burnt so we are going to eat outside, come lets go, let's celebrate auntie's birthday."

Both the families raised a toast to his mother and to our future that day.

CHAPTER 2

Nick was getting far busier in the summers than he ever was during the school. I could hardly see him in his house; he was always out for something or the other, gymming, running, swimming, playing football with our seniors who were preparing for NDA. He was so busy studying during the nights that he even forgot the fact that I lived right across the street.

"Why are you always in a hurry Nick?" he was catching his breath from a jog and I stopped him right before my house. "There are still two more years before you are actually giving NDA, what's the matter with you? You hardly talk to me these days," with my hands crossed, I was so mad at him; demanding an explanation.

"Aisha do you even see me, I have to be physically at my best before selections, I know I would crack the exams but being physically fit and mentally agile is the most important and I need to inculcate these habits in me, it's going to take a long time and that's why I don't even want to waste a single day doing nothing," he said in one breath while bending down and holding his waist for some air.

"Alright Mr Nicholas Martin, do as you please but when you are left alone in the school now owing to the fact we are in different sections now, don't even come to talk to me, ok!" I walked away furiously.

"Aishaaaa listen, Aisha"

"Don't you dare talk to me now," I went inside my house and banged the door hard. I didn't step out of my room until dinner.

"What's he doing here mom?" mom called him again for the dinner, aar-rghhh.

"Eating with us, what else," my mom completely ignored the fact that I am her daughter and she should take my side no matter what.

"No, you are not going to eat what my mom made, you go back to your stupid football friends, they will serve you dinner."

"Aisha, behave yourself."

"No mom, why do you always have to ask him for dinner, can't he eat at his own house, as it is we aren't important to him."

"Aisha watch your tongue or just go to your room." My mom would take no tantrums.

"It's ok aunty, it's my mistake, I should apologise to her."

"No betaji, she is like this only, always seeking attention, eat your din-ner; she will come back when she is hungry." I can't believe my family was having dinner without me; they were treating him well and me as an outcaste. So I was all the more sullen and hungry as well so I thought it's better to take some fresh air rather than sulking in the room.

Just when I left the main gate, Nick called me from behind, "Aishaa, stop, listen to me, I am sorry." I started running away from him and he fol-lowed me.

"You can't outrun me Aish as much as you want," now he was testing my patience.

"You bet, just because you workout and all don't show off okay. And don't talk to me and why are you running after me," I couldn't speak much while gasping for some air.

I started running faster but my home slippers were not apt to this be-haviour and suddenly I was jolted by my hand and pulled back, an over speeding car missed me by an inch, he was honking like crazy and maybe cussing; I couldn't hear because my heart was thumping as it would ex-plode.

"You stupid girl, you stupid crazy girl; have you totally lost it aisha? What the fuck were you thinking running like this amidst all the cars, you could have got hurt had I not pulled you back." His eyes were bloodshot red. I had never seen him getting this much angry.

I could have retorted but I was scared as hell, from the car that just missed hitting me and from Nick's eyes which were scarier.

He pulled me across to the sidewalk; did not even look at me and started walking towards home. I was walking behind him with tears rolling down and he was holding my wrist so tight that it was hurting but I didn't say anything; I knew I was wrong showing such reckless attitude.

The 10 minutes that I walked back home while he was walking in front grabbing on to my wrist as if I was a child who would run away, one thing I was assured that I am important to him. I was not just a friend for him, the way his eyes were blood red in anger; the way he shouted whereas I had never seen him raising his voice.

Something changed in me in those 10 minutes.

I was not the same girl.

My heart had been moved.

Even when my wrist was hurting badly; I didn't want him to leave my hand. I never felt this. This was absolutely new to me. What was this feeling, the feeling of dew touching the grass; sending shivers down making me have goose bumps on my skin. I couldn't contemplate what was happening to me, I couldn't look at him either, and he wouldn't just stop.

He stopped right in front of my doorstep and tried to shove me inside, "You don't have to be so rude," I started rubbing my wrist when he finally left it to breathe.

"You don't think, do you Aisha, had something happened; what would your parents go through, do you even care about them, do you care about me?"

"I… I am sorry" I looked at him; his face couldn't have been stiffer asking me to reflect on my actions.

"You don't have to be sorry, but can you please mind your behaviour a little more sincerely and think before doing anything, I have already lost my mother, left my friend behind, you and only you Aisha, I don't want to lose you now." There was some wetness in his eyes but he did not wanted to give away that stern expression from his face until I feel guilty about what I just did.

Though I was feeling guilty but I just wasn't ready to accept that all was my fault, "why do you even bother, as it is you have no time for me, do you even remember the last time we talked properly, you are just so busy with yourself."

"So you would just run out on streets like maniacs in the middle of the night, is this a sensible thing to do on your part."

"No, it wasn't, ok; I am sorry. I wouldn't do it again."

"Listen Aisha, you are really important to me, I might not be able to talk to you or give you time but trust me, I am doing all this because I want to achieve my mother's last wish as soon as possible and I want to show you as well what I am capable of. But please never ever do anything like this; I beg you Aisha, I can't see you getting hurt; please will you listen to me now?"

"Alright, fine, do as you please but you do remember we are starting school tomorrow and the holidays are over so we will be seeing each other daily now; or you don't wish to see me."

"Aisha; not again"

"Alright, as it is we are in different sections now so why bother," I was turning inside.

"I am going to eat with you in lunch break, I have already asked aunty to send extra," he was trying to tease me again.

"Ya whatever!"

"And by the way I have asked dad to buy me a cell phone, do you want one, we could message each other even when you are busy somewhere."

"No Aisha, I don't need a phone"

"Or you can ask your dad to buy you one."

"No, I won't do that and I don't need a phone, now go inside Aisha."

"Alright; good night"

"See you tomorrow morning"

"Whatever"

The next morning he was sure waiting for me. His uniform seemed to be tight maybe because of all that gymming he was doing, his biceps though not big but clearly visibly from the old white shirt he was wearing, he kind of looked handsome for the first time. I mean I had never seen him like that or imagined that he could look handsome or maybe I never thought of him as a man but now my eyes had changed for him and that made all the difference. I was feeling shy in front of him for the very first time. I couldn't sleep the whole night thinking and replaying all the dialogues' he said to me the previous night and they made me blush. The fan was on full speed but I was still feeling so hot that I was sweating in my bed; the way he held my wrist was making me toss and turn. So I just gave up on sleep, got up early; had a nice shampoo, blow dried my hair, ironed my uniform which usually my mom did so she was shocked a little bit and she was curiously eying me while I put on the little make up I had that means a kajal and a lip gloss; that is all I knew how to put even till date I don't know how to use anything more than that. Girls inadvertently want to look good in front of someone they like.

"Wow, someone is looking pretty"

"Does that mean I don't look pretty every other day?"

"You are unexplainably mad"

"You are looking good yourself but you might want to buy a bigger size for your uniform now."

"Yes I will have to," and we both laughed all the way to school.

Sitting in different classes for the first time I realised how badly I wanted to see him; the time until lunch break seemed so long as if it was never going to end and I was looking at my watch every now and then when Avanti nudged me with her sharp elbow, "what's wrong with you, this is our first class, why are you not paying attention."

"I am just feeling a little hungry"

"What, already?"

"Yeah"

The lunch bell sent me running to the cafeteria and seeing it empty made me think that why am I behaving so thick. Eventually everyone came, Avanti sat opposite, "why are you not eating; you were so hungry; I thought you would eat the whole café by now," and she started munching on herself when Nick came and sat next to me. I opened my tiffin and he started to eat from it. Avanti was eyeing us all along and I guess she finally couldn't contain herself, "are you guys dating now?"

"What? No." I blurted out while Nick was silently eating his favourite paranthas.

"Don't lie Aisha, I know you since we were 10, you were never so excited for the lunch break and just look at you two; anyone would know."

Nick was still gorging not at all bothered by the comments made by her as if she didn't even exist for him.

"Would you mind telling her that we aren't?"

"What?"

"What what, are you even listening or you are just interested in my tiffin?" now I was getting mad. I couldn't wait for the break to see him and here is just sitting and eating.

The bell rang and he just went, "thanks Aisha, I'll wait for you at the main gate after the school is over."

"See, he didn't even say bye to me," Avanti gave me foul looks.

"Huh, seriously this boy is something, yesterday only we were fighting on this. Look at all these boys." I pointed fingers at the guys sitting around us and ogling us; hearing this turning to other sides like lunatics and he barely looked up from food.

He was waiting for me at the school gate and we went back home together. This was pretty much our schedule for the rest of the time in the school. We going to school together and coming back, having lunch from my tiffin but that was it. Our classes were different so we wouldn't see each other except for events or annual or sports day in which he was all together a different animal now, participating in all and winning most of them as if his life was depending on these stupid certificates and medals. Once he never used to speak to anyone and no one else bothered but now he was one of the famous boys in school and girls were like butterflies around him always trying to steal a chance to talk to him but he never had time for anyone and at least that made me happy. I and Avanti would bitch about the girls from Science section who always had some or the other problem that could be only solved by him.

We would still do family dinners and he would wave good night to me from his window every night and I would feel a tinge that why does he not want to spend more time with me; does he not like me or does he like anyone else now. All these stupid thoughts would cram up my brain space and obviously I was feeling close towards him day by day but because he chose everything else over me so I wouldn't dare tell him that I have developed feelings for him.

Sundays he would come and talk to my mom; God knows about what because they would completely shun me out even if I wanted to eavesdrop; I couldn't hear a thing.

In that year it felt to me that everybody is keeping me out of their plans and he especially he, whom I helped in his initial years to settle down would keep so many secrets from me.

It was all so enigmatic to me.

But I did not wanted to stop him and argue with him because for what he was doing all this was his mother's last wish and I guess I wanted to be that one person with whom he could share things when he wanted to not because of any force.

I started paying more attention to my classes and books. I had to prove to my parents that the choice I made wasn't wrong, I needed to get somewhere from here; I wanted to know the path I would trod on. I would spend more time with my books than I ever did; started reading more nonfiction and classic literature instead of the love stories I usually used to buy. I read so many biographies and autobiographies to inspire me to be something; to make myself useful in this society and the world. I don't know how people come to decide that what they want to be; for me it was as difficult as to count the stars. Is it not okay if I have no passion; is it not okay if I don't race to become successful; will the society not accept me if I just want to live my life without getting degrees from topmost universities; I guess no one would want to be friends with me if I earn nothing in my life. Some people have this phase in their lives, I too had it.

I don't know how time passed, it crawled, walked, ran or flew, but somehow almost two years of high school passed like this and it was time for our 12th boards but before that we had the most important event of our school life and that was our farewell. In Goa, farewell was celebrated with utmost zeal and in a way it looked more like a carnival. Every school here wanted to make it so enchanting that the students never want to leave Goa. Months of preparation by the school management and junior students would go into arranging the most spectacular events for the farewell.

My dad bought us farewell gifts as is the tradition here, he bought two cellphones though not expensive, they were simple keypad phones. Nick never agreed to take gifts from us but this was a farewell gift; he would not be able to refuse.

I went to his house and kept the phone on his bed a day before our farewell; he as usual was out for workout. I could see how much busy he had been that this guy's room was messed up with books, dumbbells and tshirts over the bed. I thought to clean it up a little bit for him. Folding his sweat smelling tshirts and aligning books with thousand pages folded; God, I hated people who would fold pages of a book; I have to tell him to stop torturing the books. I wonder how my mom did all these chores without complaining ever. Salute to all you women out there.

I had charged his phone before keeping it on the bed.

Just when I saw him turning up from my window, I sent him a message: hi.

When he reached his room; his phone beeped. He looked here and there confused; sweating profusely. I could see him looking tense and now holding the phone to see where it came from.

I again texted him: heyyy

Now he looked at the phone where my name must have flashed, I saved my name in his phone as 'the nosy neighbour'

Now he looked out of his window, still perplexed holding the phone and waving it to me, questioning with hand signals.

I texted him again: why are you playing dumb charades when you can message me back. Huh.

His eyes were slightly crooked at the corners demanding explanations about this so he texted me back: what is this?

It's a phone, dumb.

Yes I know it's a phone but what is it doing in my room?

It's a farewell gift from my dad.

I already told you I don't need a phone.

You can give it back to my dad if you don't like it but it's a farewell gift and it's considered offensive here to return farewell gifts so your choice.

And I looked at him through the window and shrugged my shoulders.

This was fun, talking through eyes and texting across the street; why did I not gift him a phone earlier; stupid me.

Now my phone beeped: but why does it say 'nosy neighbour'?

Mischievously I texted him back: because you think we are nosy neighbours and we pry into your business that's why you avoid us no.

He sent me a text and closed the window: alright, I'll accept it for now but I will pay for this to your dad once I am selected. Bye.

He just said bye, no talk to you later or take care, then I thought he's new to this he might not know the rules of texting yet.

I gave up on this texting debacle and went to bug my mom for a saree. We were supposed to wear sarees for our farewell tomorrow and I had none so the last escape was mom's wardrobe.

"No mom, this is not good, no; not even this one, uhh." I was taking out sarees from her wardrobe and rejecting them one by one.

"What do you exactly want to wear," my mom was getting irritated seeing that I am making a mess out of her clothes.

"I am looking for a simple saree mom, why do you only have such heavy and bridal kind of sarees; don't you have anything elegant?" I rejected one more and threw it on the bed.

"What do you mean by 'elegant', you think my collection is not elegant enough? All the women out there are jealous of my sarees whenever I go out to weddings." She was getting furious.

"Yes I know mom and you look really beautiful in them; like out of this world but this is not a wedding, it's a farewell for God's sake and I need something subtle please help me find one mom which does not have any rhinestones, diamonds, patchwork, gottapatti or anything; a simple border would do."

"Ok I get it now, see this one then, I usually don't wear this one," and she bent down to the farthest corner of her almirah and pulled an old bag out of which came the most stunning saree I ever saw.

"Wow mom, where did you hide this one, it's so gorgeous and why don't you wear this one?" I was examining the tiniest details on the saree. It was a lucknowi chikan saree with a tiny border on which phulkari was done but it had that smell that it was buried in a grave for years.

"Because it's white in color and we don't wear white; it's a bad omen and I don't know why your dadyji bought me a saree this dull right after our wedding, he was posted in Lucknow then." She gave a sigh as to feeling nostalgic about her wedding. This saree must have brought many memories to her.

"Mumma this is not white exactly, it's a pale creamish beige, this is in trend these days, haven't you seen all the actresses on the tv wearing this color." I was in love with this saree now but it had to be dry-cleaned first and I have to hurry.

"Thanks mumma, I love this and I love you, going to get it drycleaned and I have to buy a blouse and some jewellery, I'll be back before evening."

Avanti's mom had a small boutique shop in Baga, so I went to her and she picked out a cute red velvet blouse to go with it and it had tiny straps and a frilly bow at the back. She also gave me jhumkas to wear with it.

I texted him in the night: have you got your suit ready for tomorrow?

I waited quite a bit before my phone flashed message from 'Nick the snob': yes and don't wait for me tomorrow, I'll be a little late, see you at the farewell. Good night.

I was feeling blue that he wouldn't see me in a saree first so I didn't texted him back good night. I couldn't sleep throughout because I was delighted to wear a saree for the first time in my life.

Mom made it extra special for me, she got a white gajra for me to tie at the end of the French braids she made for me; wrapped the saree with remarkably perfect neat and sharp pleats.

"No mumma, I don't want a flying pallu, tie this in small pleats," I was absorbed looking myself in the mirror.

"Where am I supposed to pin it, your blouse practically doesn't have sleeves, do you want me to tie this border to those flimsy straps," she was speaking holding the pins in her mouth.

"Yes anywhere but let this blouse be seen"

"You want to show cleavage, don't you?" mom was aghast.

"Haww mom, no, it just.."

"What haww, I know all you girls, want to show off skin like those actresses," she threw up her hands as if giving up on me.

"No mom, but it looks more pretty this way no, maa please."

"Fine whatever you wish, today is your day," and she tied it the way I asked and I examined myself in the mirror to see the best version of me.

I turned and twirled for her while she clicked some pictures in our camera, "take care beta and have fun," she kissed me on the forehead.

I glanced at his house before leaving but he was nowhere to be seen.

Avanti and I entered the school ground together where all the arrangements were done. We literally turned heads. She was wearing a black crepe saree and got her hair and makeup done. All the boys be it our class or juniors or even the teachers, they all stopped doing whatever they were busy with and looked a good minute or two. I knew we were looking incredible but my eyes were only searching for him.

The farewell tent was tastefully done in Amber colours and a chic stage complete with a dance floor and DJ. There was starters and coffee being served to us while the juniors started the function with some songs lined up with a play and a band performance.

I saw him entering when the function was almost going to end with just the titles to be conferred and the farewell speech. He had put in some efforts by wearing a nice black tie suit; I don't know where he got it from but he was absolutely looking handsome. I tried to stare at him but he absconded to the farthest corner.

My name was called for Miss Charmer and I watched him clap for me. By the time lunch was over, it was almost evening and time for the best part of the day, Farewell dance.

All the lights lit up and we were admiring the beauty of our school building with tears in our eyes that we are soon going to leave this place. This building has so many memories, our hearts and souls into it. The dance floor was occupied and the students were going crazy dancing to the latest bollywood songs but I just wasn't in the mood. Avanti dragged me to the floor when our favourite song 'desi girl' started playing and I had to dance for her. All the guys gave us the centre space and I could see Nick talking to one of the Science girls in the corner and I got so agitated that I danced hard just to make him jealous. The creepy boys whom I had avoided all my school years thought of it as a chance to hit on me and they started dancing really close to me. One such freak tried to touch my waist; by the time I could push him away he had already groped my back and was pushing himself on me. It all happened in a flash, I saw Nick swimming through the crowd; pulling that guy by his shoulder and punching him hard in his right eye. That guy instantly fell on the dance floor and everybody was astonished and froze to digest what just happened. Nick pulled me by my wrist just like the other day and hurried straight out of the school ground.

"What are you doing Nick, just leave my hand."

"You are hurting me Nick, leave my hand, I can't walk this fast in a saree, stop ok." I screamed.

"What is wrong with you?" I jerked my hand.

"What is wrong with you Aisha, dancing like this with those idiots," he argued back with a stiff questioned face.

"So what, it's my choice as you chose to speak to those over smart girls of your class and did not even bother come see me, why did you not come with me this morning?" I folded my hands and demanded to know.

"I was getting my suit ready and something else.." he babbled something in low voice; I couldn't hear because of the music coming from inside.

"Sorry what, what else?" I went close to him to hear properly.

He looked me in the eye, "Aisha there is a place I want to take you; will you come with me?"

"What place?" I was still scorned.

"I'll tell you," he turned his gaze from my face.

"Ok but first lets go and dance, don't spoil it; I have waited for so long." Inside slow romantic tunes were playing and all the couples of the school had taken the centre spot, singles were just ogling them and trying to find themselves a partner.

"Come no" now I tugged on his hand and took him back. The scene was normal now, that guy was taken away and everybody was just absorbed in the moment. We progressed through the crowd and oh boy; I thought Nick would be a novice but he was a pro at couple dancing. With his strong arms he rotated me with such elegance, held my waist in his palms and danced like I had never seen him before. "Wow, amazing Nick, I never knew you could dance fairly well," I was shouting in his ears.

"By the way you did not even tell me how I am looking in saree."

"You are looking spectacular Aisha, just like your title; the most charming," he screamed in my ears.

The night was going terrific until my ankles got sore with the new heels that I was wearing so I removed them and sat in a corner and watched Nick; now dancing with Avanti. I never knew he could be such a charmer if he wanted to. I always knew him as a shy boy; never thought he could be so manly and punch someone for me. I was elated in my heart and I was asking myself what this new feeling was.

After a while, Nick came and picked up my heels, "Do you want help walking?" he joked.

"No thank you, I can walk, let's go home" I held up my saree from falling on the ground.

"No we are not going home," he stated.

"What do you mean we are not going home, its 9 already, everyone will get worried," I was unsure about what was happening.

"We have to go somewhere, I told you; come let's go. You can wear my shoes if you want." He stopped to look at my feet.

"No, I'll prefer walking barefoot."

"Ok then I'll also walk barefoot."

"Your shoes are perfectly fine." I exclaimed.

"Ya but then you would look stupid walking barefoot alone," he took out his shoes and held them in his other hand.

We were moving like this, me grabbing my saree so that it doesn't get dirty and he was carrying both our footwear. "Where are we going Nick? Till how long I have to go on like this?"

"Just 10 more minutes; we are almost on the beach."

"What? Beach, why?"

"Sshhh… can you remain silent for like two minutes Aish."

I didn't utter a word until we reached the beach.

The sound of crashing waves could reach us now, it was absolutely dark and scarce; the heavy damp air was all around but not a single soul where we were escaping, the last point of the beach. I could get glimpse of some light at the end and to see it clearly I surpassed him and I was awestruck. There were scattered rose petals and lanterns on the sand. I stood there in astonishment. The simplicity of the beach and enchantment of the petals and lanterns took no time on me to register that something massive is going to happen. I froze with my hands on my lips and my saree flying and getting spoiled by the sand. He came in front of me and just stood there, looked at me and nothing else. I looked back in bafflement. We might have stared each other for so long forgetting everything else until the lanterns went off and it was absolute silence and pitch black, I could hardly see him now. He came close and took my hands away from my face and tried to jolt me out from the scene.

I looked into his eyes now; still unable to open my mouth. My curiosity was at its peak.

"Aisha, I know I have been a jerk towards you these days but that's just because I want to fulfil my mother's last wish in the best possible way and I want to show your parents that I am worthy enough for you. I don't want them to think about me as just any other boy goofing around in life."

"I love you Aisha."

"I was a completely different person until I met you; one with whom no one would want to attach themselves. I did not have confidence in me forget about reaching to this point where I am now. You knew me back then and still you chose to be my friend even when I pushed you outside my life, still you stood there for me, you chose to stick around. Had it not been for you; I don't think I would have survived all these years alone. You encouraged me to do things, you were the motivation I looked on to everyday, and I became a better person because of you; I groomed my personality for you."

"I owe you everything Aisha and you mean the world to me."

He got down still holding my hands which were trembling by now, "you have solved the puzzle of my life, will you always complete me like this Aish, and will you forever be mine?"

My ecstatic impressed face with a smile that could touch my ears and tardy tears that were now rolling down through my chin. I couldn't assure myself that it was seriously happening with me. There was no way I could have anticipated this. This guy who hardly talked to me in front of people, who avoided social contact; who might have never seen a bollywood movie or read a romantic novel planned all this out.

I was out of my senses with excitement that I forgot to answer him and just kept looking at him that this might be just a dream from which I was about to wake up any minute.

"I am still here Aisha," he coughed.

"Oh shit, I am so sorry, shit, sorry, no, oh no, no sorry, I mean sorry," I went down on my knees to face him where he was already kneeling.

"I never imagined any of this Nick, I never thought you would like me, forget about loving or proposing to me, I am just terrified that you planned all this."

"Aisha will you be mine forever?" he cupped my hands and rubbed them for some warmth.

"Yes, of course yes, a big yes, a very big yes," I couldn't contain any longer and my gleeful eyes filled with tears.

He pulled me towards himself with insane speed so that we could hug just like that on the cold sand while kneeling. As if he was waiting for years to hug me like this. I cried on his shoulder; he sobbed on mine. We were both so alive and weepy at that moment. He got up; pulled me up and again we embraced each other just like the world is going to end here. We stood there for long with eyes closed and listening to each other's breathing which was synced by now. My bangle clad hands at the back of his shoulders and his firm palms on my bare waist. This moment was so surreal; I was fully absorbed in him when he pulled himself a little back; took his hand from my waist and placed it at the end of my chin, made me look up at him and placed a kiss on my lips. It was just a brush of lips. He looked at me, I quivered a bit; I closed my eyes in anticipation and he kissed me again. This time a little more and a little deep, I wanted to kiss him back so I clenched my fingers around his neck to pull him closer to my face and I stood on my toes so that I could come up to his lips. We kissed and hugged until we heard the siren of police car which was patrolling the beach at midnight. We ran back to home; he was still not wearing his shoes and carrying mine as well. We reached home panting and giggling; having the best night and knowing that we love each other.

I did not want to let go of his hand; neither did he. We kept looking at each other holding hands and trying to part our ways but let me tell you its way too difficult when you have just expressed your feelings for each other. We could have stood there all night long jamming our knees and getting cold but I heard my mom coughing inside and I knew she is still awake; waiting for me. I pulled my hand back, gave him an apologetic smile and made my way inside the house.

I silently scurried to my room upstairs, changed as cautiously as I could so that I make no noise and slipped inside my bed. I took out my phone to text him:

I can't believe I have a boyfriend now ;)

While I was waiting for his text, I heard mom's footsteps so I hid the phone inside the comforter and acted as I was asleep since when. She checked on me and went to her room. My phone beeped:

I am not your boyfriend Aish, I am your partner with whom you will date, love, marry and grow old together.

Oh boy! This boy is surprisingly getting romantic and raising all the standards I might have set for him. I had butterflies while reading his text.

Alright partner Nick, let's sleep now. Good night.

I love you partner Aish. Goodnight.

I dozed off to sleep with so much contentment that when I woke up I saw mom hovering over me.

CHAPTER 3

I sat up straight with my brain alarmed trying to recall what wrongdoings I have done for which I was about to get scolded.

"Did you even wash your face or fold the saree before sleeping?"

Oh the saree, I looked down on the floor where it was lying down in a complete mess, I gave her a reassuring look that I would do it right now.

She was eying me all this time; mothers know everything that is going inside out, I looked at my face in mirror with horror; all the smudged kohl and lipstick was already hinting what transpired the last night.

"We danced a lot yesterday maa, I was sweating like anything."

"I came in early only; you were sleeping that's why I dint wake you up."

"Beta I have already been at your age years back, don't try to fool your mother." She grumbled.

"What do you mean maa?" I went to wash off my face first.

"I know you were with Nick." She came and stood behind me in the washroom.

I had just filled my mouth with water which I spat on the mirror hearing this. "Sorry, what mom?" I turned back.

"Nick had already taken permission from me yesterday after you left that he wants to surprise you and take you somewhere, where did you go?" she had this pleasant face when one already knows that the other person is lying.

He had the audacity to tell my mom that he was going to propose me. Amazing! I was feeling embarrassed in front of my own mom for lying. It felt that they both have teamed up again against me. Why would he want to tell the world before confessing it to me? I felt a loss of words. What should I tell her? We had awkward silence until dad came upstairs and he shouted, "So how was your date Aisha?" I looked at him in horror; he also knows that I went with him, wow! I gave both of them an unacceptable nod and ran out of my room straight to his house and his room where he was still asleep. This was the first time I had seen him sleeping, look how cute and innocent he looked in sleep while doing such outrageous and devilish things without asking me. I came here to shout instead I got all lovey dovey for him but still I had to vent out my anger.

"Get up you fool," I removed his blanket as to terrorise him.

He sat up wriggling and rubbing his eyes, "What on earth happened Aisha?"

"What happened, you are asking me what happened; why did you tell my parents about all this." I literally growled on him.

He started yawning, "So you are mad because I told your parents."

"Yes and who knows you might have blabbed about this to everyone in the school; our street; bloody all of Goa."

"Stop right there Aisha, I have just asked your parents' permission and wasn't it the right thing to do before taking you anywhere?"

I gave it a thought, maybe he's right but I can't accept my defeat just like that, I have to come up with some counter argument, "but why does everyone has to know that you love me even before I did."

He got up and pulled me by my hand that I landed on his bed, he kept his palm on my mouth, "Ssshhh Aisha, I told you that I want us to be a forever couple, that's why I confessed to your parents first, they are family Aisha. They should accept me first."

I was feeling hot lying next to him looking into his feisty eyes, pleased with the explanation that he gave, I tried to move out from the bed and just like a gentleman he let me.

"What else have you told them so we both are on the same page Mr Nicholas Martin?"

"Nothing else Miss Aisha Singh, definitely not about our kiss," he winked.

I went shy at the very mention of kiss and clenched my lips to control the smile, "bye I am going," I scurried off.

I was embarrassed to face my parents but nonetheless if he had the courage so should I. "Mom I love him," I pretended to be casual about it while looking here and there.

Both of them laughed incredulously, "We already know betaji."

"Yes everyone knows; does our milkman know about it, you should probably tell this to him as well."

I went to my room and texted 'nick the snob':

For future reference, I should know everything first.

Yes, nosy neighbour. Came the reply.

We started dating right before our boards and that meant not much time for the relationship. There was no school but it was worse because in school at least I would see him and he would eat with me in the lunch but now all he did was to lock himself up in the room with his precious books and the minimal we talked was through messages but that too was limited because he wouldn't use his phone and I didn't want to protrude.

On my side studies were easy because that's what I always used to love, reading and reading, all the characters and scenes and narration would directly go to my heart of every play that we read in school so much that there was even no need to revise it. I was the only one in our class who would find the hidden meanings of verses and the actual messages that the authors wanted to spread across the world. I wasn't petrified of the exams now because I knew my stuff and this is massive plus point for anyone if they know what they are doing and they love what they are doing, life becomes easy, you have fun doing everything. Your daily routine doesn't bore you or fills you with thoughts such as I could have chosen something else or I could have done better, you tend to feel satisfied in every realm. I was satisfied with the choice I made; it's just I still needed to figure out where this was going to take me.

We would exchange good morning and goodnight messages everyday. We kept our windows open so that at least we could see each other through, and wave and shout something cute.

On Valentine's Day we mutually decided to chuck studies for one day and spend time with each other.

I texted him first: Happy Valentine's Day. Can you wear something nice today, I want to click pictures.

After the usual wait he texted, Happy Valentine's Day sweetheart. Yes, got a new black shirt yesterday and got something for you as well, do you want to see it now?

I jumped from my bed and screamed from the window, "show show"

He held a red colour tunic in both his hands and it looked so lovely. "Wait, I am coming. Give it to me now, I'll wear this only." I sprang from the room to his house, kissed him on the cheek, took the dress and came back.

We decided to meet in one hour. So I straightened my hair and put on a nice perfume over the tunic he got me and in exact one hour, he was waiting at my door.

"Wow Nick, you look great in black. By the way your forearms are getting bigger day by day." I touched them in awe.

"Aisha this was a top, you were supposed to wear jeans or something underneath," he continuously stared at my bare thighs.

"Oh, I thought it's a short dress. Do you want me to change?"

"No, you look great, if you're comfortable let's go like this."

"Good answer, even if you would have asked me to change, I wouldn't have done it anyway. I was just testing you."

"So did I pass?"

"Ya with flying colours," and I held his broad forearms tightly.

"But you do know that you are really fair and this red dress is making your legs look flashy white and maybe everyone will just look at you."

"Oh thanks for the compliment Nick the snob."

"That's how you have saved my number right just like you put nosy neighbour in mine?"

"How did you guess?"

"Intuition"

"Does it still say nosy neighbour?"

"Check for yourself," and he handed me his phone.

He had saved my number with the name 'my life'. I got so emotional seeing that, I looked him into the eye, "isshh so cheesy but i love you Nick" and I hugged him tight.

"Aisha, our neighbours are staring" he coughed.

"Oh, let's just walk to the beach, oh wait lets go to that Marimba Café on the beach, they are hosting a Valentine party or something.

The café was all donned in roses and heart shaped balloons and there were couples everywhere holding hands and whispering sweet nothings to each other. I just loved the vibe there. So much of love in one frame. It's only possible in Goa. There was a local band playing some Irish songs on the Guitar. All the tables were already occupied so we sat on the rock cut bench near the palm trees facing the sea. He was moving his fingers on my hand.

"Why did you confessed your love so late Nick? You could have done it a year earlier at least we could have dated for that long now."

"I don't know Aisha, it just didn't feel right to me, and even now also I had to gather so much courage. Otherwise I thought I would propose you once I am back from the Military Academy."

"Are you kidding me? Thank God, you said it now. What if I started dating someone else while you were gone?"

"If we are meant to be together, we would have no matter what Aisha." He put his other hand on my dress which was flying because of the high tide and winds.

"You know, you are very old fashioned but good you told me before going. By the way how long would you be gone after the exams?" I was most concerned about this.

"If I get selected in the exams and interviews and medical tests which will take about two months for the whole process to be completed and results to be declared, I'll be gone for 3 years Aisha." He was looking at the sea. Maybe he wanted to avoid my face while saying this.

"3 years!"

"You'll be gone for straight 3 years Nick?" I was sounding desperate now.

"No you fool, of course I'll come back during the leaves, and the Academy sends back its Cadets during the four week off twice a year in June and in December." He smiled at me reassuringly.

"Ok so June and December, that would be our time and we would celebrate Christmas and New Year together."

" I'll look forward to it because I'll get to see you, meet you, and touch you." And he touched my cheek. "You are turning red Aish."

"Aye, stop it."

"See you are getting goose bumps Aish" and he touched the back of my neck.

"Aye Nick, stop it no." I ran off to the shore.

He ran after me and held me from the back, lifted me up in the air and tickled me. We were both laughing hysterically.

"Promise me that you will text me every day and call me whenever possible," a slight faint tear was forming in my eye.

"I can't promise you, what if one day I am unable to do so then you'll be hurt and I don't want to hurt you ever. But I promise that whenever I am able to, calling you would be the first thing on my mind."

"Alright"

"But you also have to promise me something."

"What?"

"That you will use your time in the best way possible and you will make your parents proud. You will make me proud, wont you?"

"Alright"

"Alright is your catch phrase no Aish?"

"Yes and you are my catch, arasso?"

"Now what is arasso?"

"Arasso is alright only but in Korean" I made a pout face towards him and he instantly held that pout with his fingers and kissed me.

He held me tight from my waist and kissed me back, because of the winds my dress was fluttering and he tried to hold it back but instead his hand slipped on the back of my upper thigh and it felt like an electric shock to me. He instantly removed his hand and placed it at the back of my head to pull me closer to his kiss.

We embraced each other knowing we just had some more days until we both part ways. We both were teary eyed, I was crying on his chest while he was dropping his tears on my shoulder.

"But I'll miss you like anything Nick, how will I live without you for so long."

"I'll miss you more, you are at least with your family here, I'll be away from all, it will be a new place for me and you already know how difficult it is for me to get into new places. It will be all the more struggle for me when you are not around."

"Aww that's cute." I pulled on his cheeks.

We giggled, ate pizza, danced to that band and drank god knows what but I am pretty sure it made us feel dizzy because we kissed and kissed until both our phones started buzzing. That one day was my go to memory. That one day will stick to my heart and soul, my mind and my body.

CHAPTER 4

We solemnly forget to enjoy the little moments that dawn upon us. We keep waiting for future places to go or events that weren't even going to happen. We fail to memorise the exact merry time that we spend, we forget its cheerfulness, we forget how delighted we were, and we fool ourselves into thinking that someone far away is going to bring more pleasure than the person sitting right beside us having just a cup of tea is our actual happy place. My happy place was Nick and I knew he thought the same about me. No matter how much we nagged each other or did not go on fancy dates but deep down it didn't even matter. The only thing I wanted was to be with him, whether it be here or anywhere in the world.

Day by day my fondness towards him increased, in a way a lover would want to see, in a way a mother would love to care, in a way a friend would want to support. I knew these exams were really important to him and that's why I didn't asked much of his time but I also knew the clock was ticking and the day would soon bomb upon us when he had to leave.

Our boards went pretty easily, Avanti and I did late night studies sometimes at her sometimes at mine. We would study till 2 or 3 in the morning and then open the main gate of our house and sit on the porch with hot coffee and talk to the watchman. He was amused by us and would stop everyday to check upon us. We would chat with him a little, offer him coffee as well.

Now when I look back, those were some pretty awesome days that I spent, I don't know where that watchman went, I don't see him now, maybe because I sleep by 10 now.

Nick would laugh at the mere thought of us doing this. But he never questioned my thoughts or decisions; he was always supportive no matter how stupid my acts were.

We got free after the exams but not him, his main test was still left; the entrance for the NDA. He had some more days to prepare for it and he gave it his all. His dad was quite worried and shared the same with my family, he thought what if he didn't make it, he thought he will get depressed and all but I told him that I am hundred percent sure that he will make it. My dad told him not to worry because the kind of dedication Nick has, he hasn't seen in anyone.

His exam was in Panaji town so he had to go there a day before. I hugged him really bad but didn't cry as I didn't want any bad luck upon him.

"All the very best Nick, I know you are going to crack it."

"I'll do my best Aisha," he sounded a little nervous.

I gave him a folded piece of paper and winked at him while he was leaving with his dad. I had written him a good luck note:

Mirror mirror on the wall,

Who's the bravest of all?

Nick Nick shouted Aisha,

The dumbest of all.

Good luck to my prince charming, you are the best, Mr Nicholas Martin and you are going to make everyone so proud.

If you pass, I'll wear that red dress again but this time when no one is around. Xoxo.

He came back after two days, he didn't say much and I was scared to ask him about the exam so I just chatted along to lighten up his mood. He was very sleepy for some days, maybe because he never slept at all during the exams.

His result was supposed to be out in next 15 days and for those days; he remained tensed and silent even for the times when I was with him. I wouldn't do anything remotely possible to make him remember about the results. Instead I would summarize the latest books I read; for him and I would tell him about the books I loved and why I loved them.

One such book that I had read recently after the boards when Nick was too busy was Memoirs of a Geisha written by an American novelist, Arthur Golden. I had found this book at an old thrift store for just 50 bucks, it was old and covered in dirt; nevertheless more the antique books, more they fascinated me.

So I was sitting with him on his terrace and he was listening to me with intrigue.

"Do you know anything about Geisha's?"

He nodded in denial. Of course even I wouldn't know about them if I haven't read the book. That's the power of reading in cross cultures and countries, they help you understand the world.

"First I thought, they are kind of prostitutes or into some sort of sex business but when you study them deeply, you will come to know that being a Geisha is a difficult job and it's a full time profession in Japan and its respectable. It will take years of practice and learning and thousands of classes for a girl to be trained as a Geisha. It is one of the oldest profession and an art form prevailing in Japan. These girls will learn the traditional Japanese music and dance from a very early age and continue to do so until they be one. They have to be always dressed up in traditional Kimono and white makeup and always smile in front of their guests which are mostly men. They can't show anyone how physically or emotionally tired they are. They have to pour 'sake' for their guests at the parlour, sing and dance, sometimes do poetry as well."

He was just nodding his head but I know he always pays great attention to whatever I say because he thinks that he can never read novels so he was always impressed by this habit of mine.

"They have to be immaculate, impeccable and polite at all times, do everything in style and panache; be it pouring tea or opening the door of tea houses. It might take hours for them to do their makeup and wear Kimono's and they walk in wooden slippers. They leave their parent's house and live in Geisha houses where they are trained and they live their whole lives like this until someone is ready to take them. No one will marry them but might keep them as a mistress in separate house but still many girls aspire to become a Geisha. Their love and sexual life is diverse than their professional lives."

"So in all I just want to tell you that no profession is lowly, in some parts of the world there will be such odd jobs that you can't even think of but they are there."

"Sounds like an interesting book" he took the book from my hands.

The day of his result was a tight one; everyone was so nervous and pale. I kept looking out of my room's window in anticipation of him running to give us the good news. He had gone to a cyber centre to check the results and my heart was skipping fast. I was praying for him, that's the only thing he wanted and honestly me too. I earnestly wanted him to go through; never did it occur to anyone of us that what if he didn't make it.

I heard footsteps climbing up the stairs and I got all jittery, he was there in my room.

"What happened Nick?"

"Tell me, you are killing me."

I was numb.

He was numb, his face didn't give away what he wanted to say, was he happy, or was he sad.

"Aisha.." he gave me a serious long face.

"What Nick, come on, why are you acting like a suspense novel heroine," I swear I would have traded anything to make him utter a word.

"Aisha, go wear your red dress," and the curves of his lips turned into a slight smile.

"Whaaaaaat!!!!" I jumped at him in excitement with my hands on my mouth.

I landed straight on him and he picked me up in the air and swirled.

"I can't believe I made it Aisha, it's all because of you. I love you so much; I can't tell you how happy I am." He was still holding the printout of the result.

"Nick, you'll be in Army soon" I had tears of happiness in my eyes.

"I still have to go through interviews and medical," he put me down.

"That will be easy as cheese for you," I took the paper and read it aloud.

I was so proud of him; he succeeded in doing what he loved the most. I wish I had that kind of dedication in my life for anything but at present I didn't.

We were about to kiss when my mom walked in and coughed and Nick got all embarrassed and instead kissed my mom on her cheek. "Aunty I have done it."

"I heard Aisha's loud voice betaji," my mom gave me a look, "I am proud of you son," she hugged him like his own son.

That evening both the families had dinner together and celebrated. Amidst all the celebration I was lost in thoughts that Nick would leave me soon. It did dawn upon me that his success meant our new official relationship would turn into a long distance one and this would be more difficult because he was going to NDA, they aren't allowed to use as much phones or visit home frequently, I knew this but I had to put up a smile for him.

"Aisha you can stop faking now," he sipped his cocktail and whispered in my ear; we were sitting next to each other.

"I am not faking anything."

"Yes you are, you can't fool me, I know when you are laughing from the heart and when not, so stop acting like a fool," he picked up a lamb chop.

"You are so heartless Nick, how are you able to drink and eat so much, I can't even gulp water at the mere thought of you going away," I turned to the other side.

After returning from the restaurant we talked on the phone.

"When are you planning to leave then?" I put the phone on speaker and started applying lotion.

"I have to first go to SSB Bangalore, it's the selection board and I have to go through various fitness, medical tests and then group debates and finally an interview. If I clear all this, then in about a month I'll have to pack and leave for the NDA Khadakwasla, Pune."

"So you'll be in Pune and I am here in Goa, approx 500 kms apart and a 10 hour journey, right?"

"Wow; nice math, unexpected from you though,"

"You don't have to be so rude, I am not that bad at maths," I put the earphones now.

"What is 78+89, fast, you have ten seconds."

"Aaaann, stop doing this Nick, fine who wrote the Hamlet?"

"Ohhh, I don't know"

"Then stop being a male chauvinist," I laughed.

"Big words, male chauvinist; where did that come from? You are reading way too much literature."

"Nick, how will I survive without you?"

"Aisha, what do you want? You don't want me to go? I'll not go."

"I am not saying that I don't want you to go, it's just going to be very difficult. We have always been together and it's more of a habit for us to see each other every day."

"It's just three years Aisha and I'll be coming in every year for the holidays and we can talk on the phone but don't expect me to write letters, I am terrible at it."

"Alright"

"And here comes your Alright"

"You will miss me?"

"Of course, there will be no girls, none hot like you, so I'll miss my girl." He was trying sarcasm.

"Oh, but I'll have many boys around here, so maybe I'll not miss you as much."

"You can do whatever you want Aisha but you'll be marrying me someday."

"I don't want to marry you; you'll be gone in the army for years just like my dad, giving no time to the family and one day you'll die in some stupid war. I want to be with someone who would live at least hundred years with me."

"You can be with me till I die in some war and then you can be with anyone who would live up to hundred, okay?"

"Alright"

"By the way when are you going to wear that red dress?"

"In your dreams"

"That's cheating, you promised me"

"That was just to cheer you up"

"So now cheer me up," he was sounding so cheesy.

"Maybe on the day you go"

"I'll leave next week for Bangalore Aisha."

"Uff too soon"

I don't even remember that next week passing by because it was such haste and commotion. My parents were busy preparing for some cousin's wedding in Amritsar for which we had to leave soon.

Nick and his dad were getting him new shirts stitched. He packed every-thing and booked his tickets. We met all our friends one last time before everyone parts their ways into different cities, colleges, maybe countries. Maybe we will not meet some of them in our entire lives. Slowly we will forget their names and how they looked and what they talked about.

On the day when he was supposed to leave for Bangalore, he came to touch my mother's feet; though he was a Christian but he knew what goes around in my culture and family. My mom blessed him in pure Punjabi; he might haven't understood a thing but as it goes; love has no language.

I was up in my room donning the red top and when he came up I closed the door behind him, "What are you doing, your mom is downstairs," he was taken aback.

"And she knows how to give space to her daughter," I shyly hugged him and put my hand behind his neck to pull him closer and kissed him with passion.

He put the bag down that was in his hand and pulled me up by waist and made his tongue go deep inside my mouth and almost touched my breasts for the very first time. I was lost in his embrace; I let down my guard and kissed his jaw line and down on the shoulder blades. We cried, hugged and kissed and again cried.

"I am not coming to see you off," I wiped my nose.

"I don't even want you to, you be here and I'll be back in a week." He took out his handkerchief to wipe my tears.

"Only to leave for 3 years. Do your best, okay." I was holding his shoul-ders.

"Yes madam" and he saluted me, which made me laugh.

"I should salute you now," and I gave him a salute, I have to learn how to salute properly first.

He pulled my cheeks which were blood red by now and also the tip of my nose because of all the crying. He loved how my face turned red due to crying or just a slight change in weather. He always loved to pull my cheeks and squeeze them hard until I cried to leave them alone. I was much short than him so he would all the more stand on his toes so that I couldn't get away easily from his grasp.

I didn't go to see him off and the next day we left for Amritsar. It was the first time I was visiting real Punjab and I carried my supply of diary and pens to capture all the memories and places. I loved to capture events, people I meet and the new places I visit through my journal, not with pictures but through my words. Wedding affairs are serious business in India. It never occurred to me how much you spend on a 2 or 3 day affair. There were cousins who had flown in from Canada and others who came from Delhi and all other cities of Punjab. The marriage nuptials were in a beautiful gurudwara and somehow it made me imagine how I and Nick would look if we would get married like this but then suddenly it struck me that he was Christian, I don't think I will ever be able to wear such a pretty lehnga.

Nevertheless, the wedding was mesmerizing and the visit to Golden temple was absolute wonder for me, it kind of made me forget a little about him. But the very next day, all the family went to Wagah Border for the Closing Retreat and then I was back to missing him terribly and imagining him in uniform one day. What a proud moment it will be for everyone when he will walk down in that camouflage uniform.

We got back to Goa before he came and my Admission letter also arrived. I had applied to St. Xavier's college for literature and arts in Mapusa, Goa. Avanti was also in the same class so the new college wasn't at all strange to me.

We did not even text or called each other during this week, I wanted all his concentration to be on his selection process.

He came back with good news, we already knew he would be selected, and there was no chance that he wouldn't get through. We raised a toast to his selection. He had to leave for Pune in next 15 days. Our colleges will start around the same time.

I helped him buy his daily needs and clothes; we went shopping for the list that was provided. It was fun to do such daily chores with him, buying simple things like shaving foam and toothpaste for him. We even fought over the color of the towel; I wanted him to buy something quirky like orange or beige but he insisted on buying white.

People these days forget how to enjoy the little moments that they can share and enjoy. One doesn't always have to look up to big dates or big trips or events and occasions to come up but everyday could be a bliss if you start being satisfied with the choices you make in life.

I also bought him a handmade diary from the lil flea market and packed it in his suitcase, "if someday you feel like sharing something; pen it down here. If some days you miss me and want to tell me something that you can't over messages and call; then write down a letter. Writing it down will make you feel lighter and content." I stood on my toes and touched his head like a mother would caress a toddler and then hugged him tight. I knew he was feeling bad but he would never show it of course. Even men feel sad and lonely, they want to cry out their emotions but they wouldn't.

"You know that I will come back after six months," he held me.

"Of course and I'll be waiting for you Nick"

"You have to promise me that you will take care of yourself when I am not around"

"I promise you"

"And you will not cry"

"Hey, i can't promise everything ok," I looked away

"Look at me Aisha, you will not cry, I'll be back in six months and this is the time where you should focus on yourself, think what you want to do."

"Alright"

"Alright" and he laughed.

I tried to learn how to bake cookies from mom. I wanted to surprise him by baking cookies which he could take along, he used to laugh on my cooking skills and it turned out to be true. The cookies were supposed to have square and circle shapes but instead they came out looking all oddly and disfigured as if I have splattered the batter all over the oven. He actually laughed on the non describable geometric shapes but said they tasted quite good, I doubt that he was telling the truth.

And just like this; the fifteen days were over and he went without saying goodbye because we both would have cried like idiots and goodbyes are always tough. He asked his dad also not to come along; these days his dad would most of the time feel sick and will never agree to visit a doctor or take medicines no matter how much we forced him to. I told Nick that he does not have to worry about uncle; we will take care of him. My mom had packed a month's supply of dry fruit Laddoos for him and he just laughed how Punjabi mothers poured their hearts out in form of food. He had left flowers and a note for me saying that he loves me and he will miss me to the core and I should stay away from the stupid boys of my college, typical boyfriend.

When he reached Pune, he texted me: 'reached the campus, it's so beautiful Aisha. Going to check out the dormitory and later for lunch. We aren't allowed to keep phones here, will have to submit it in the locker. I can only call you through the STD booth here. I miss you already.'

I texted him back: 'happy to hear you loved your campus, go and eat properly, make some friends, sad to know you can't keep phones. Alright call from the STD whenever you can. I miss you too.'

Why did he not tell me this before that he wouldn't be able to keep his phone, maybe he didn't wanted to upset me more before leaving.

My college was similar to all other art colleges, 10:3 ratio of girls to boys and lecture halls empty but canteens full. Professors would just give us entire books to read and submit our analysis and detailed character essays. Just two girls in the class would do the file work and rest would copy, those two girls were me and Avanti.

I waited for like 3 days for his call but he only called me on Sunday.

"Aish, how are you, I am sorry I couldn't call"

"Where the hell were you, why didn't you call?"

"Aisha we are only supposed to make calls on Sunday, we can call during weekdays if it's an emergency but here I am hardly getting time to sleep, forget about making a call."

"How are you?"

"I am okay baby but the regime here is very tiring, if it's not for the hooter bell at 5 am, I don't think I would even get up. The whole day we are hooked to something or the other till evening, just the second I hit the bed and I doze off."

"Baby? Learnt a new word?"

"Everyone here calls their girlfriends baby, babe, what do you want me to call you?"

"Babe sounds good but first tell me; did you talk to your dad?"

"Yes just called him, but he didn't say much."

"He's not been feeling well, my dad pursued him to visit a doctor but he denied as always but don't worry he is eating all meals with us and mom also made some herbal medicines for him."

"What would I do without your family Aisha, I can never repay your parents."

"Hey, stop Nick, we are one family. Do you miss me?"

"I miss you the entire time babe."

"So we will only talk on Sundays?"

"Sundays are confirmed, I will still try to call in between if I can, this is the common STD booth so I can't take up much time and we have one landline in every squadron. I will try to call you from there, say hello to your mom and dad and tell mom that her laddoos have made me a ton friends here."

"I love you Nick and I miss you," I was now trying to control my shaky voice.

"You are my life babe, I am nothing without you, I'll call you soon, don't worry and don't you dare cry, bye sweetheart." And the phone got disconnected.

It felt like a pang, the beep tone that was still going on my mobile indicating that we will now talk after one week made me realise how difficult this is going to be.

I joined a local magazine of Goa as an intern to kill the evenings when I was extremely bored. They asked me to write up an article on spot and were amazed at my writing skills. Being good at vocabulary and literature, they easily hired me on a minimal stipend of 5000 but still it was great from earning nothing and sitting idle all day.

I would rewrite the articles written by the journalists who were on the front taking interviews and examining the daily events in Goa. I would edit them and give more clarity and depth to the written pieces and would help the photographers to choose the best capture for the written piece.

Basically it was a desk job, I even got a work laptop from them to edit all their content even at home. My mom was so happy to see the laptop, "you have earned a laptop with your talent beta, I am so proud of you."

"It's not my laptop maa, they will take it back once I leave their office," I would correct her.

"But still till then it's yours, no one your age has got a laptop with their own abilities, maybe with their parents money but not because of their own talent," she was brimming with joy.

I was waiting for the coming Sunday to tell Nick about all this progress. I fully charged the phone and kept it close even in the bathroom so that I don't miss his call.

And it rang somewhere in the noon, I grabbed it fast in a heartthrob, "hello, Nick, can you hear me? Are you there Nick?"

"Aisha, I missed you, I missed you a lot baby."

"I missed you so much stupid," I was shouting in the phone so much that my voice could have reached Pune without the phone.

"I love you, I love you, I love you babe," he ranted back.

I hugged the phone and kissed it as if I was kissing him instead, "how have you been, are you eating properly, you are not sick or hurting any-where right?"

"Sssh Aisha, I am alright, I eat full 3 meals because if I don't I would collapse in the middle of the day. The exercise regime and training is de-manding and harsh, some boys have fainted in the beginning only."

"It's just two weeks that you have gone and I feel so lonely Nick."

"I know it feels so long that I haven't seen you and it's going to be a long time until I come back home. We have to get through this together baby."

"I wanted to tell you that I have joined Chronicles Magazine. They hired me as an intern to edit and write behind the scenes. They are paying me a stipend of 5000 and also gave me a laptop; I could take the laptop home so that I can write in the night." I was bragging about.

"Wow, Aish, amazing, see just two weeks that I left you and you are al-ready doing so much. I always knew I am eating up your precious time when you have so much hidden talent."

"Don't say that, it's because of you that I am able to write so much. I miss you. Come back soon." My voice got heavy.

"Just 5 months and two weeks for this semester to end and I'll be home."

"That's not 'just.'" I rolled my eyes on the phone.

"Okay, I have to keep the phone now baby, the queue is getting longer."

"I'll wait for next Sunday," I cleared my throat.

"I love you, bye" and the phone got disconnected.

Every time he would disconnect the phone so abruptly, I would be left asking for more the whole day. Unlike others; Sundays were going to be tough on me.

"You look like you haven't slept the whole night," said Avanti examining my face closely as a doctor would do. We were sitting in the front as usual and she was holding my face; looking for the signs of sleeplessness.

"Hatt Avanti, everyone's looking at us, they as it is think we are lesbians."

"Let them think, good na, they wouldn't bother us with their stupid gifts and proposals," she grinned. "But tell me why you aren't sleeping properly?"

I tried to avoid this conversation but she was reluctant, given the status of my girl bestie, she would never give up until I tell her.

"I think he has got along with his life there and he has completely forgotten about me." My gloomy face was saying it all.

"Why would you say that?"

"Because for the last two weeks; we have just talked for not more than two minutes. How do you think I am able to put up without talking or seeing him for so long?"

"Kya Aisha, I thought your love is above all this nonsense long distance issues."

Her comment hit me hard.

"Hmm, maybe you are right, am I over thinking all this?" I looked at her for some guidance.

"Yes you are, there is not one guy whom we could compare to Nick in terms of trust and love that he has for you and his passion to join the army. Not a single boy in our school was as dedicated as he was and here you are still questioning his love?"

"I am an idiot; no?" I felt guilty.

"No you are just a sweetheart who misses her boyfriend too much, but you have to let go Aisha, you can focus on your career and let him do what he always wanted to and anyways he will come back soon."

After the classes I straight went to the Chronicles office and sat down at a round table with three more interns from different fields like photography, marketing, sales and content creation. Rohit, Jishaan and Sanchi respectively were my new friends. All three of them were older than me and were working here before me so they had more experience and hence they always wanted to see my work before I submit, take me to lunches and also the guys asked me out but I had to let them down and tell everyone about Nicholas who had joined NDA.

"Again an all nighter," asked Sanchi looking up from her laptop.

"Nope not really, couldn't sleep properly." I brushed away further questions and started working on my recent article given by Sunita Mam, she was the chief editor of the Magazine, who took my interview also. She asked me to write an article about the increase in drug intake by local college students and it was easy for me being the daughter of a police officer whose specialisation was in busting drug rackets and rave parties. I took his help in determining the causes and reading his old case files. I went to a rehabilitation centre also where such youngsters were being treated for dropping out of schools and colleges due to drug addiction. I felt heartbroken seeing those young kids spoil their lives. Some were treated half way and they volunteered for my interview and promptly answered all questions.

The marketing guy, Jishaan; he had such a flabby personality, always trying to delude me. "Boss is looking for you," he looked at me creepily from his laptop as if I weren't wearing a shirt.

"Thanks, I'll go and see her."

"I think you should first grab a comb, Ma'am doesn't like unkempt hair flying randomly in her office."

I put the strands behind my ear and gave him a sharp Gaze, "Pardon me with your unsolicited advice Jishaan, Ma'am didn't hire me for my hair but for my articulate writing skills."

He returned to his laptop and I retired in Sunita Mam's cabin.

"Morning Mam" I sheepishly stood in front of her.

"Morning Aisha, I wanted you do an interview with 'Sapphire Band' and its lead vocalist Sandhu or as people call him Sandy."

"What? I mean you want me to do an interview with Sandy, The singer Sandy?" Sandy and his band were one of the most impressive cult bands and he was going to perform in the music fest in Goa. To meet him personally is a thing I never thought of.

"Yes, I don't see a problem in that."

"No Mam I meant that I am just an intern."

"So you always want to stay an intern?" she had wrinkles over her spectacles.

"No, but this is something really big and I don't think I'll be able to pull it off myself." My palms got sweaty.

"Look Aisha, I do recognize the incipient talent you have, you just need a little push; that is all what I am doing."

"Alright mam; I'll do it."

"Decent"

I rushed outside to announce this great achievement to Sanchi and others.

"Wow, seriously, you are going to meet Sandy, please take an autograph for me." Sanchi's voice was loud enough for everyone in the office to hear about it and they all flocked to my table when Sunita Ma'am came out with a thunder, "what is this turbulence all about? Go back to your work, fast." She clapped her hands like a ring master and all the zoo animals on their desks.

I was scheduled to meet the band next day at 9 am because they would get busy after that for rehearsals. So I reached hotel Grand Hyatt early that day, skipping breakfast. I picked out a nice and plain black pencil skirt and a maroon blouse to fake a famous and busy journalist carrying all my supplies, notepads, colour pens and a recorder if I missed something in writing, I could later add on it and a big questionnaire handed to me by Mam herself.

I asked the reception about the band and entered my details next to the visitors slip. The band was having breakfast in their suite so I was asked to go up to their suite on the 7th floor.

When I rang the bell, a half naked guy with dreadlocks on his face opened the door and yawned at me, he was reeking of alcohol.

"What the hell, you guys don't understand or what. We are sleeping, first you come to put breakfast and now what, came to take it back?"

"I… I am here to take interview…. Interview." I shoved my notepad in his face to make him realize I am not from the housekeeping. Stupid junkie.

"Oh, okay, sorry, please come in. mind your steps though."

It was a bizarre place, they must have just spent the night in this suite and what havoc have these guys created, it looked like this place got raided and the room was damp with the smell of cigarettes and alcohol, puke and what not. The furniture was all hay-wire. The half naked guy came outside wearing an orange colour sleeveless t-shirt and I instantly recognized him as the drummer of the band.

"Sorry about this mess."

We tiptoed in the room being careful not to fall on the numerous bottles lying down and I sat on the couch. In front of me was a three layered breakfast trolley and my stomach rumbled so hard that even he heard it and laughed, "help yourself, I'll wake them up."

I placed my stationary on the white marble centre table and picked up a croissant.

I was munching on it when Sandy came outside from the bedroom wearing nothing but star printed Boxers. Having weird multiple tattoos on his body and piercings at unimaginable places.

"Comfortable?" he asked me.

"Yupp" I nodded and lied.

"You are actually on time," he wanted to see the time on his wrist but he wasn't wearing any watch so I helped him, "its 9:30, we were scheduled for 9am."

"Oh! Sorry, my bad. Can we do it like this or should we all get dressed?" he was scratching his stubble.

"However you feel like, I am not taking any pictures, it's just a recorded interview, for pictures, our photography team will come in the evening during the fest."

"Okay, let's do it now, boys come out fast." He sat beside me.

It looked like a scene from porn, 5 guys showing most of their skin circling around me.

"I'll start with you," I turned on the recorder and took out the questionnaire; asked him the first question.

"Your real name is Sandhu Bajwa, what's the story behind 'Sandy'?"

He raised his eyes ferociously as if I trespassed my boundaries on the very first innocent question.

"My girlfriend used to call me that; she cheated on me while I was just struggling and decided to run off with a wealthy NRI. I wanted to get famous so that bitch would curse herself for leaving me every day but now this name's just stuck with me though personally I don't like it when people start screaming Sandy Sandy, then I only see her in the crowd."

I never knew this hunk of a guy could have this soft side as well.

"How did you came up with this name 'Sapphire' for the band and how did you guys decided to start performing together as a band" and all other questions went smooth enough. They seemed to be genuine people only with bad habits. They were more than eager to help me with all questions and asked to have breakfast with them. I took his autograph for Sanchi and promised to attend their performance in the evening; they gave me 4 VIP passes as well.

I worked that whole day to finish writing the entire interview to be printed in the magazine. Refined it, edited it until I collapsed in slumber. Woke up drooling, realised I was running late for the show. I took mom, dad and Avanti went along. They were watching a music show for the first time and got impressed that I had the VIP seats. I missed Nick, wished he was here with us to witness all this.

Stress was evident on my sleeping cycle and hence Sundays I preferred remaining in my bed all day long.

CHAPTER 5

My phone was vibrating vehemently under the pillow, barely was I able to open my eyes and saw the time on my alarm clock, 4:30 am, pitch black outside. I thought who's calling me at this time.

It was an unknown number but anyway I picked it up seeing missed calls from the same number.

"Aisha, where are you? I was calling you from the past half an hour." He was growling from the other side.

"Normal people sleep at this time Nick," I sat up rubbing my eyes and wiped the drool over my face.

"By the way whose number is this? It's an unknown number and I don't pick unknown numbers, people are troubling me these days." I had to tell him.

"What? Who's troubling you Aisha? God, why would you not tell me about this?"

"No one in particular; just my number got circulated in a WhatsApp group in office; as well I don't know who's been texting or calling me, so I don't bother answering unknown numbers or replying to texts."

"You tell me whose number is this? And why did you not call me last Sunday, I was waiting for your call the whole day. Also how are you calling at this time?" My brows rising demanding to know.

"We have been brought to a training camp Aish; in some jungle; to be isolated and trained how to be self sufficient. We have to gather wood, start our own fire, find fruits, vegetables, whatever that is available here. We have been chopping wood and finding things to make a temporary tent, this was for our survival if we get posted or stuck in arduous and untenantable conditions. We were brought here last week without any prior notice, so I couldn't inform you about it and some of the seniors have sneaked in their mobile phones but there is no network here. I was trying to find the network here and but no luck, the call wouldn't connect. I knew you would be waiting for my call today so before anyone else got up, I have climbed this steep mountain and I'm standing on top of this mountain to talk to you, only here, I am getting a faint network. I will go back down when I'm done talking with you."

"You've climbed a mountain at this time, just to talk to me. Wow, this is a real love story like seriously you are crossing oceans and climbing mountains just to hear my voice." I was still yawning. "I hope you don't get scolded for this."

"I will get punished for this if I am caught I know but then it's okay, I knew you would be waiting for me and I couldn't talk to you from past two weeks so now tell me how are you babe?"

"I am good, just got busy with college and office as well. In office, some of the guys; they have started giving me so much more work than I could ever handle because they've come to know that I write much better than them so they are trying to shove their work on me plus I had to go visit the rehabilitation centre with dad. My sentences gushing out with slumber.

"You are working hard baby."

"Yes it was really busy for me but still I missed you every night. How many months have gone by and I don't know how and when are we going to meet," I was looking outside the glass window and my voice started breaking.

"We will meet soon Aisha; we've taken this so far. Already two years have passed and just one more year and I will be back," his calmness assuring me.

"Oh and I wanted to tell you that your dad is clearly unwell these days. He doesn't eat anything all day long. We tried to make him eat but all he ate from the past few days was just a bowl of daal and little bit of rice. He has stopped reading his newspapers as well; whole day he's just lying on bed and looking out of the window. My dad forced him to visit the hospital but he declined. We called the doctor home to get his check up done but then he shouted on the doctor that he did not wanted to get any check up done and asked all of us to leave him alone."

"What? I did not know about this, I wasn't able to talk to anyone from the past few days and the last time I called him, he didn't answer the phone."

"Yes please call your dad right now and you take care of yourself. You don't have to climb mountains or go anywhere just to talk to me I am here only waiting for you. I'm not running anywhere; your Aisha is here waiting for you to finish your training properly and come back like a hero. You get it Mr. Captain?" I convinced him everything is fine.

"Yes Mrs. Captain, I get it. I will call dad now."

"I love you Mr. Captain"

"I love you more than my life Mrs. Captain," and the phone clicked. We had started addressing each other like this, the sound of 'Mr Captain' felt so alive.

I couldn't believe my ears that just to talk to me he has climbed a whole fucking mountain. Have you ever seen a love story these days where just to talk to each other people do such things. Today people want sex more than love but mine was different. It was more than everything.

That night his father had a stroke.

He died in his slumber, peaceful death in sleep.

When I went to his house in the morning with the breakfast because he skipped the dinner also last night, I was ringing the bell but there was no voice. Usually he would call out, come in, it's open or something but today there was no noise at all. It was all calm, I got quite nervous and the door was locked from inside so I couldn't open it as well. I leapt back running to my house shouting that something's wrong, the door is locked from inside and he's not answering or opening the door. We knocked on the door several times. I also called out from the window but there's no sound from the house. We banged the doors and windows, my father tried to break the lock of the door but it was jammed. So he went to the backyard of the house and broke the black window pane of the kitchen.

My dad pushed aside the broken glasses and jumped inside and rotated the knob on the front door so I and mom could also get in. When we went to his room he was lying on his bed peacefully. No sign of life but no sign of struggle, pain or discomfort on his face. My dad looked for his pulse but it was long gone, his body turned cold and pale.

He looked at us and nodded his head to confirm what we were thinking was true.

I started crying, how we would tell this to Nick. He would be shattered. It's his last year of the training and we don't even know their other relatives. What would we do? It was all in shambles. We called the doctor who lived in our society; he came quick and announced that he was no more that he might have died in the night in deep sleep. Therefore there was no sign of movement or discomfort.

I came back to my Room grabbed my phone and quickly dialled the number from which I had got the call on Sunday. For long I tried calling that number, called 100 times but it would not connect. My dad knew some people at defence Academy in Pune so he called them up and asked to relay the information to the team who had gone for hiking. Till the time Nicholas came to know about this, our neighbours had gathered in the house because we weren't Christian so we didn't know what and how to proceed with things and we needed their help in arranging the last rites and when Nicholas called back in two hours on my number, it was a landline number showing.

He didn't say much just informed us that he's going to take the next train and will reach Goa by midnight and asked us to wait for him and not do the funeral Without him.

We did not know how Christians did their final rites. Our neighbours had called the Father of the King Luther's church in our society because there were no direct or close relatives that we knew and the pastor suggested that we should do the funeral today itself, everyone pitched in that keeping the body for one whole day is not a good idea but I was against it. We told them we will have to wait for Nicholas; he had requested that we do not do the funeral without him. My dad requested the pastor, "that's the only thing he asked for father and he the only family he got, how can we do it without him?"

The neighbours were coming in-and-out from the house whole evening, my mom didn't come out of the kitchen, she hid herself behind preparing tea and meals for everyone; she feared watching the body again and again. Some of the men helped clean Uncle and made him wear his black suit that was hanging in the wardrobe. The coffin was ordered.

Everything seemed to stop in front of my eyes; I was unable to decide what to do? How would Nick react, what would we tell him that we couldn't care for his father properly, how would we console him?

There is no way one could sympathize with him; he lost his mother when he was young and now he lost his dad too while he was preparing for the only dream he had in his life. Why is life so unfair to some people?

Nick's train was running late, he came in early morning. He came straight to his dad's room and dropped the small duffel bag that he was holding on his shoulder. We were all standing there, crammed up in the small room but it still looked empty because the owner of the room had left.

It looked that he had cried a lot during the journey, his eyes were blood red. When he saw his dad he just sat down, held his hand and said, "why now dad? why now? I needed you the most right now. Just one year was left for the training. You would have seen me wearing the uniform of Indian Army.

Why dad why? Why you also had to leave me?"

He was breaking apart while saying this; he banged his head on the corner of the bed where his dad was lying. My father came and stopped him, he didn't say anything. The neighbours started saying we should leave for the funeral procession now because it will take time to get to the grave-yard and for the burial process and after that the funeral service also has to be done so we should leave.

Nick cleaned up and wore a clean black shirt, he avoided looking at me. I did the same; I had no heart to look at him. The funeral cortège started and I was behind; trying to hide behind people. I did not even look up and I did not came close to him while he was crying on his father's death bed. I did not wanted to see him like this so I was just walking behind though my mom and dad were walking with him.

Unlike our community's rites where we are supposed to wear white, here everyone wore dark colours for the funeral procession. There were around forty people of our neighbourhood. We reached the graveyard soon, the Pastor was already there. They slowly lowered the coffin into the already dugout grave. Six feet under the soil interred a body which was breathing until yesterday. People started pouring the soil with their hands on the coffin and the Pastor was reading something from The Bible. "Corinthi-ans 5:8, we are confident, I say, and willing to be absent from the body, and to be present with the Lord."

Nick was shovelling the gravel on the grave and repeating pastor's words in mumbles, his lips were moving but there was no voice. I don't know how he was holding up without a single tear. Why was he controlling himself, he should let out those tears. It was like the life was taken from his face, no expression, no grief, no pain. He was trying to be brave on the outside but I know how vulnerable he was inside.

The internment burial took about an hour and slowly the people got sparse. We went to the church behind the pastor for his final funeral ser-vice, usually it is done after some days but because nick asked the pastor to do it today so that he could go back to his training; everyone agreed and we headed towards the church.

This was the second time I had stepped inside a church, first time Nick only took me there last Christmas, it was different then, was so much more lively and joyful. Now it felt like a whole new place where there were no bells chiming, it was utter silence. The big domes felt huge and empty, there were wooden rows for people to sit and read the bible. We occupied just the two front rows and there was a small picture of his dad and a candle burning before it.

As a eulogy, near ones and relatives were to speak about him but only nick and my family were the close ones so my dad offered to speak before nick.

"He was a brave man, I have never heard him complain about anything in life, not even the pain he was bearing, he hanged in there till his last breath, he was alone but never asked for anyone's help and he was a strong pillar for all of us in all these years. He had a remarkable personality and discipline; I know he must have reached heaven by now. We will miss him; he was part of our family. May his soul rest in peace." And he came back and sat next to Nick supporting his shoulder indicating that he should go up to the aisle to offer his eulogy now.

He was grim, absent minded and reluctant to go but somehow gathered himself up and stood in front of us.

"Dad, this is what I called him though I was closer to my mom but after her death he was my only family. The only person I could look up to but he decided not to tell me that he was sick, maybe he didn't wanted to bother his own son, maybe he did not wanted to get treated in the agony that his wife couldn't be treated, maybe he wanted to suffer in silence. I wish he would have at least talked to me, the last thing I heard from him was a frail little 'I wish I could have saved your mother.'"

"I couldn't say that I love you dad, that I miss you, that I will be back soon and we will together go to the church for mother's death anniversary and that we will go for fishing and boating as was his dream. I couldn't do anything for you; you did not give me a chance dad. I hope now you have met mom above and finally you both are happy leaving me alone like this here. I love you both, please be together now wherever you are."

He touched his father's photograph and a tiny tear trickled from his eye which he instantly wiped away as if he didn't wanted to show that he is in grief.

The father said the prayers and while we all had closed our eyes and joined hands in unison to pray, Nick decided to leave us.

When I opened my eyes, he wasn't there, I looked around the rows and entrance of the church, but I couldn't find him anywhere. I hurried outside the church at the cemented footpath and the garden but he was nowhere to be seen. I asked some people who were coming in, had they seen a boy in black shirt going out from here, someone had seen him going towards the main road. I rushed towards the end of the street and I slightly caught a glimpse of him boarding a bus. It was bus number no 4, heading towards the station, he was carrying the duffel bag he came with. I waited for the next bus and got down at the station. I asked at the enquiry counter if there was any train to Pune and if a boy in black shirt had bought a ticket. He didn't know about him but told me that a train to Pune via Mumbai is leaving from platform number two.

I was gasping from sprinting so much still managed to climb the stairs and looked at the train which started moving, the wheels were slow but they were gaining pace and the engine driver was blowing whistles. I ran as fast as I could shouting Nick Nick, because I knew he was running away from me, from us, from his home, I fell on my knees, he was going far from me in this train and I couldn't catch hold of him.

I was kneeling on the platform, crying incessantly, asking for the train to stop, asking Nick to at least talk to me once before leaving, to share his pain with me but he decided against it. The train left the platform and all I was left with tears and just a glimpse of him during the funeral service. Will he come back, will he call me, and will he reach safely to his academy all these questions started haunting me.

People were staring at the way I was bending on the floor holding my head and tears dropping on the platform. Someone asked me if I am okay but all I could see was the blurry vision of the train leaving.

Dad had followed me to the station, "Get up Aisha; what are you doing here?"

"He left, He left dad; didn't say a word. He did not see me even once, just left."

"He will come back beta, he left because he wants to be left alone, he did not want any company or to speak to anyone, we men are like this only, we never share our pain and tears with anyone. He will get better in time; you need to give him some space Aisha." Dad pulled me up from the ground and held my hand to take me to the car.

I kept looking back; even the train was gone now.

Days, weeks, months passed. I never got a call or any message from him.

I thought he was angry with us,

That he won't forgive us for not taking enough care of his dad or was he just avoiding me, does he thinks of me as an incompetent person. But we did the best we could. All these thought kept me restless and resulted in interrupted sleep and foul mood every day in college and office.

I begged dad to call his academy, though we came to know that he is there doing his training but he rejected taking calls from anyone. He denied taking any leaves or outings and just stayed in the academy until his training would be completed.

CHAPTER 6

It was almost eight months that I didn't hear from him, though he was the first person in my mind every morning and in my dreams every night.

I used to sit in my room near the window looking at his house and thinking about the times we spent in his room, at his terrace and just like this; looking at each other from the windows itself. All my essay reports and projects for those eight months were half hearted; it felt useless to accomplish anything without him. For me, he was the only motivation I had but now unsure if he is ever going to come back to me or not, all I wanted was to hide myself in the bed and cry out on my pillows. Mom dad were really pissed off with me, trying to talk some sense into me that he will come back as soon as his training got over or we will go there once it's done. That he just needed some time to grasp all this. But I wouldn't understand, I stopped eating much, gave up on going out with Avanti and even deleted all the Korean series that I had and wanted to watch. Because these romantic dramas would make me miss him all the more and I hated whenever I saw couples anywhere.

One morning when I thought of cleaning my attic and utilise my day instead of whining over everything but my mind was somewhere else, the dress which I wore on prom was hanging at the last spot of my cupboard, made me nostalgic and I hugged the dress imagining I was hugging him at the beach.

"If it pleases miss, can this handsome man over here be hugged instead of that dress?" I heard some voice from the door of my room and turned around to see Nicholas standing there in the army uniform with two big shoulder bags and a smile that I haven't seen in the longest of time.

God, he was here.

I leaped on him and held him tight thinking this just might be a dream which could vanish in an instant so I should seize the moment. But no, he was there, really there, I don't know how, but he was here in my arms.

I pinched his cheek to confirm that it's not a dream.

"ouch slowly aish," he exclaimed.

Hearing this 'aish' in his voice sent shivers down my spine.

"I will kill you, I will really kill you or kill myself if you are again going to disappear like this," I grabbed his collar.

He placed his hand on my mouth, "enough of killings babe, no more deaths please, I want to live with you."

"So finally you are back right? Is your training over?" I questioned looking him in the eyes.

"Yes I am back for good, can't you see this uniform. I signed up to become a Para Commando." He took a step back to show his uniform.

And God, wearing the uniform of Indian Army, he looked a completely different person.

"I can't tell you how difficult the training was," I knew he had a long story to tell so I was all ears to him.

"For 12 weeks we underwent the toughest training of the country, be it physical, mental or emotional; they tried to break us in every possible way."

"But I did not give up Aisha," he seemed to tear up a bit thinking about those days.

"There were nights where I cried, I used to miss you so much, and I missed mom and dad so much. We couldn't tell this to anyone; we couldn't make any calls. We had no phones; we were not being fed properly. That was the time where they see which cadets can become the Para commandos. They do this in order to check what our limit is, what is our breaking point, where we will give up the training. They try to find that one thing which will break us the most. We ourselves come to know about our saturation till where we can take the stress and pain."

"I never got more than 2 or 3 hours of sleep in the nights." He held my hand; I wanted him to take it all out so that it stops bothering him.

"The last two days of the training were like an exam, only 12 of us cleared through it. They call them the 36 stress hours. I can't even imagine now how I went through those stress hours."

"They used to wake us up in the middle of the night with gunshots and alarms and then we had to do our fitness regime and activities where we had to pick up weights as much as 40 kg and walk up a steep Hill. You would come down and again do ground exercises and do circuits taking up more weights than your own body."

"For 36 hours, we were only given one glass of water and a packet of food. We were not allowed to sleep or take any rest in between. Then they took our mental examination to check our operational tactics and observation skills. There was so much pressure but we tried to do the best we could perform. I think this is the highest level of training that any possible human could undergo." He must have waited for so long to tell me all about it.

"I am so proud of you Nick, I don't know how you have gone through all this but I know one thing that you are the strongest man that I will ever know in my life; I love you Nick and I always believed in you no matter what comes, you will become the man your mother wanted to, you wanted to, this was your destiny, it was waiting for you and I'm so happy for you Mr. Captain." I kissed his hands which were all cut and rough.

"Yes Mrs. Captain I wasn't scared from all this but I get scared in front of you. That day when I ran away, it was because I couldn't look at you, I was scared to even talk to you. I could never let you see me like this, devastated, hopeless, a coward."

"I knew that you were coming behind me, I am sorry Aish that I didn't stop, I am sorry that I didn't say anything to you but I wasn't in the state to talk, I was just angry and I didn't wanted to let that anger vent on you."

"You don't have to be sorry cappy," I caressed his forehead.

He kissed my palms back. "You know Aisha; I could only survive because I feigned anger and ignorance towards those hostile days and kept waiting to be with you again."

"You are the only person who makes me go weak, I can't see you getting hurt; I can't see you in pain, I can't see you crying, I can never see a drop of blood on you Aisha." His gaze pierced me.

"I missed you cappy, see I have Goosebumps just hearing what you underwent, I never thought it could be so inhumane, such arduous conditions and I thought I was the only one in pain without you." I tried to stop my tears by looking up.

"When I got that maroon beret, that moment I was the most contended, that now I am the part of Indian army's parachute regiment, a Para SF commando. I was wearing the maroon beret for which I have been trained hard for so many months. It was finally the time where all my blood and sweat was giving me my dues. I wished you were there to see me wearing this," he handed me the maroon Beret.

I held it in between my hands, touching the soft maroon fabric on the Beret, underneath lies months and years of his tireless and zealous efforts, the time that he lived away from all of us, from his dad still.

This was his reward, I looked up at him, "I love you Mr. Captain, you are the most worthiest of this Beret, you have already made all of us proud, look there, your mom and dad are so happy." I pointed towards the sky.

"Maa, I did it," he showed the Beret towards the sky.

"Let's get married." He said nonchalantly.

I was helping him clean his house and the broom from my hand fell on the floor, "what?"

"Let's get married," he thought I didn't hear him for the first time.

"Is this how you ask a girl to marry, nick?"

"How would I know, never asked a girl before and no one has asked me for marriage," he smiled.

"Is this some kind of a joke," I got agitated.

"No its not, I am asking you to get married to me, why would it be a joke," he turned away and started cleaning the other side as if this is what he does every day.

"So this was how you were going to propose me while I am holding a jhaadu in my hand," I picked the broom up and threw it at him.

Gosh he did catch it.

He came after me, picked me up and made me sit on the dirty window slab, held both my hands, all my efforts to fight him were in vain.

"Aisha, I love you and I might not be able to become the hero of your fictional novels but I am sure I am going to love you and care for you more than them. All I need is you right now to be with me forever, day and night. I don't even want to waste a single second to live without you. I have spent enough years without family and now I want a family. For that you will have to marry me Aish."

I laughed at the baby face this captain was able to make.

"We can live together without marriage also," I suggested biting my lower lip inside.

"No, not happening. I want you till death do us part, not a second less."

"Awww, look at my Captain; getting so serious," I laughed and winked.

"So it's a yes or no?"

"First let go of my hands," I demanded.

He placed my hands around his neck slowly, "is it better?"

"Best"

"Now, will you marry me?"

"I am already yours Mr Captain, we can get married now, if you want," I kissed him on the cheek.

He tilted his face and touched my lips, wrapped his arms around me and stood in the gap of my legs and started kissing my lips. His eyes wandering over my mouth as if he was looking at my lips for the first time and touching them slowly; just when his tongue touched mine, I heard mom's rambling.

"Eeww, we are so dirty and mom can look at us from her kitchen," I pushed him a little.

Immediately he backed off hearing my mom could look at us.

Now it was my turn to tease him.

"So what now, are you going to talk to my parents?"

"What, me?" he stammered.

"So send someone from your commando team to talk to them, okay?" I was having fun teasing him. I just loved teasing him, it was the only way to look at his innocent puppy face.

"Aisha, I can't do it alone, let's go together and talk to them." Now he was my subordinate.

Ohh what a great feeling it was, "Absolutely not, you will have to talk to them yourself."

"Baby please, please I request."

"Hmm I can help you but on one condition," I crossed my arms and put up a serious face to scare him off.

"Tell me, I'll fulfil all your conditions."

"I know we will have to do a church wedding but I seriously wanted to don a lehnga all my life."

"So wear your lehnga"

"Where? In church?"

"That would look awkward"

"Forget it, its okay, as long as you are by my side, I can do without a piece of clothing," I hugged him.

"So you are saying yes to our simple church wedding."

"Unless my parents say no."

"Gosh, I have to deal with a full Punjabi family; God save me." He laughed and I punched him on his forearm.

It felt like the first time when we walked back to our homes from that park, we were holding hands and he was looking at me with those shiny eyes which had dreams of us being together. He let go off my hand, once we entered the kitchen where maa was busy kneeding a dough; we were cooking butter chicken and naan for dinner. It was going to be an unusual dinner.

"Mom, Nick has something to tell you." I walked straight to her.

He gave me looks with raised eyebrows and questioned me with his expressions that how could I speak so casually about something so significant.

I was having the time of my life, so I just sat down on the lounge chair next to the kitchen door looking at Nick and mom.

"what is it, tell me beta?" my mom stood next to him reassuringly which made him even more nervous.

"Auntie umm aa.. I mean maa'" Nick started stammering.

I laughed out loud sensing that he won't be able to speak.

"Mom Nick has just proposed me for marriage so he wanted to take your permission."

Nick was aghast, he thought that I have committed some kind of perjury, if I could have said it so casually; I should have done it in his place.

My mom was confused and she looked at me and then Nick, I am sure Nick was sweating at that time.

"Maa I really love Aisha, I promise you I will never Hurt her or let anyone hurt her. I will never let a single drop of tear come out of her eyes. I love you guys as much as I loved my parents and I promise to take the best care of her; I want to marry her as soon as possible; I want to make all of you my family, will you be my mother?" He bent down in front of her and I thought, he should have bent in front of me first. Huh.

I looked at the two of them, my mom blushed as if getting proposed for a second marriage. "So the day has come when I'm finally getting rid of you," my mom turned to taunt me. I told you my mom was savage.

"Thank god betaji you asked, I thought you would never ask to marry her and she would always be piling on us; she never spares a minute to us; we don't have any privacy."

It felt as if mom was ranting and complaining to Nick about how much I have irritated them. "Mom please, I never interfere between you guys."

"Nick get married to her right now and just take her away from my eye-sight."

"Maa"

"What maa?"

Now Nick was having his time watching us two quarrel.

"Okay okay stop it you two, mom, Aisha; please stop it. Can we not do it like this in front of Dad please." He literally begged us.

Mom was really happy, she couldn't stop thinking about my marriage. Me and Nick were lazing off the whole day in my room; just reopening some old albums; laughing how chubby and cute I was as a child.

"Look at your tomato red cheeks Aish, so fluffy I would have eaten them if you had them now." He pulled both my cheeks until they turned deep red.

"You can eat something else now," pointing towards my lips and tongue, I winked at him showing him my naughty side for the first time.

"Oh ok ok babe stop it, your mom is downstairs and your dad will be home any minute. Sober up. We need to talk to him as well na." He squeezed my face and kissed the tip of my nose.

When dad came, everything was perfect; the mood was set with warm lighting and light old school bollywood songs playing on maa's radio. Dining table full with Punjabi food, mom dressed in a nice sari and Nick also changed into fresh clothes and the three of us were sitting on the dining table. Dad thought something's fishy here.

We took him for surprise.

"Okay I know something's been cooking between you guys, come out clean with it; I can barely digest the food. Tell me what do you guys want to say?"

Mom made the first move, "He proposed her, so let's get them married soon." My mom was jumping with excitement.

Dad looked at all of us with disgust, "you think marriage is some kind of joke, you think it's as simple as butter and cheese. Can you get married just like that without thinking about your future. How are you going to support each other; have you thought about your life. You both are just 22-23, is this a proper age? I think you should both focus on your career's first." He started eating and we were all taken aback, scared as hell. Dad was never like this. What happened to him; what got into him?

I looked at mom and Nick. All three of us didn't pick up a single bite from our plates.

After a long pause, after scaring the shit out of us; my dad laughed, laughed bad, burst into a span of laughter.

"Gotcha"

"All of you" and he pointed fingers at us.

"You thought all of you could fool me with this nice food and everything, I also know how to pull a prank." He was laughing with the butter chicken gravy dripping on his beard.

My mom shouted at him, "Amrinderji, look at them they are at the verge of crying how can you pull such a prank.

"Are I am sorry betaji, i was just pulling your leg. of course I am more than ready for your marriage." He got up and patted Nick's back and kissed my forehead. "I couldn't have asked for a better son-in-law; I know you are the best for her. She is still a stupid child, forgive her for anything she does."

"So let's start preparing for the marriage and functions, and we have to call all our relatives and decide on guest list, marriage Hall, Halvai, decorator and we also have to go to Mumbai to purchase her lehengas, we won't get good stuff here in Goa and we have to call our Panditji from Amritsar." She spoke without even catching a breathe.

"Have you forgotten maa that Nick is Christian."

Her face got pale, she felt loss of words. "okay so no Punjabi wedding?" she questioned with some hesitance.

This was her dream from the time I was born to throw a big fat Punjabi wedding and seeing it going down the drain; she was the worst hit.

"It's okay however they get married, their happiness is more important to us not how they get married." My dad talked some sense into her.

"No maa, we will do it as you want," Nick turned towards her and held her hands.

"Papa look at them, looking like Jaya Bacchan and Srk OF k3G." I was busy eating my chicken.

She was elated and that is what mattered in the end.

"That way you can wear your lehenga na Aisha," winking at me while hugging maa. It was a full Hindi movie drama scene.

"I suggest let's do a dual wedding; Punjabi and a Christian wedding." I finally got up from my chair and hands down firm on the table like I have made a final decision, "that way I to get to wear Lehenga and a wedding gown as well."

All three of them looked at me thinking how greedy I am but why not if you're getting married do it the way you want.

"Alright as you say," Maa gave me a nodding smile, "but that will increase the expenses," my father added.

"My mom interrupted, "Please don't think about expenses, I have saved a lot for this day; ek hi beti hai Amrinderji." Mom and dad agreed but Nick looked a little sad, "I don't have that many savings," he looked down. I sensed his uneasiness.

"You don't have to worry about it beta, just give us the numbers and address of your relatives and friends; we will get everything done," my dad again patted his back. "I don't have any relatives that I know; never contacted any. I just have one old friend back in Mumbai and some from the Academy," he didn't smile much saying that.

"Okay we will invite them all." My mom said reassuringly, she had already started planning things in her head.

Wedding bells were ringing for us soon; without wasting any time we got married in two weeks. The whole affair was simple and intimate; surrounded only by families. We didn't invite a huge crowd, only close relatives and from Nick's side there were only three of his friends. Our paternal relatives came all the way from Amritsar and they left no stone unturned to fulfil all the tasks we usually do.

For the two days before our church vows, I was dripping in besan and turmeric more than the onions. Nick used to laugh looking at me; telling me, that I'm turning into a Samosa. He had never seen so many loud aunties at one place who were always singing and always eating, singing, shouting, eating and snoring. He was staying with us only because we had put all of our Amritsar clan in his house while he was more than happy occupying our hustling and bustling space chuckling at the sight of my torture and binging on the sweets and savouries he's never tasted before.

When I was getting my mehndi done, he stood at one corner of the living room and watched me. From far I could see his eyes tearing up with the thought of us getting married a day after and finally some happiness in his life after a long ruthless journey. He came to me with a glass of lemonade while my hands were henna laid, pushed some loose strands of hair behind my ears, wiped the sweat from my forehead with his Kurta which my mom got him and pushed the straw in my mouth, all this while looking at my mehndi with close observation.

He did it in front of my relatives, they looked at us in some unapproved way. My father's elder sister pushed him to move aside taking the glass from his hand, "aise ni vekhte kudi nu" and they all chuckled on Nick getting sheepishly pink and leaving when he understood he wasn't allowed to see me or my mehndi.

All my aunts went crazy wild thinking about their own marriages and complaining that their partners haven't cared for them like this even once in all these years. Just to think of it, I felt contented that he cared and loved me so much that it is making everyone jealous.

So everything was in budget, instead of booking a hotel; we rented a villa for two days and everyone stayed there with the mandap being set up in the open near the pool. The first day we did a Christian wedding according to their culture, we registered our marriage the same day.

He was dressed in a crisp black tuxedo, clean shaved with his handsome features and broad shoulders he was looking no less than Korean actors. He was accompanied with his friend as his best man to the church where the marriage registrar was already waiting. I didn't buy a gown or a Lehenga, that would be wasting huge amount of money. Avanti's mom being a designer knew many other big shot boutiques in Goa who rented wedding attire so we got great discount for both my dresses. It was avanti's mom who made my mother go against her wish of going to Mumbai for wedding shopping after she showed her that in one tenth of that price we can get nice outfits here only. See we Punjabis do spend a lot of money on weddings but we are also smart enough as when it comes to save it.

My wedding gown was an elegant mermaid style strapless bodice, it was a pale ivory colour with a diamond studded belt at the narrowest waist to enhance the curves of my body. My aunts did a collective, "Hawww" when they saw that my cleavage was fully visible through it. They tried to cover it with letting my blow dried hair fall over my shoulders so that at least I get some coverage. I let them do their way because the only thing I was waiting was to see him. I have waited forever to be his.

With a bunch of white tulip flowers in my hand and my dad escorting me inside the church, my walk down the aisle was a really emotional one. All the guests on both sides of the aisle were cheering for me and in front of me stood Mr captain, looking like a true Captain.

He couldn't take his eyes off me, he saw me gleaming in that gorgeous gown and all that wedding glow on my face. It was marking the start of our married life. He was left speechless as I neared him, he took out his hand to help me climb those two steps to stand besides him in front of the priest. You wouldn't believe but my punjabi clan was quite as a dough while the vows took place.

The priest did some readings from the Bible and asked us to take our vows. Nick preceded me, "I, Nicholas Martin, take you, Aisha Singh, to be my wife, to have and to hold from this day forward, for better, for worse, for richer, for poorer, in sickness and in health, to love and to cherish, till death do us part, according to God's holy law, in the presence of God I make this vow."

"I, Aisha Singh,, take you, Nicholas Martin, to be my wedded husband, to have and to hold from this day forward, for better, for worse, for richer, for poorer, in sickness and in health, to love and to cherish, till death do us part."

After making our vows, we exchanged rings, these simple circular rings which have no beginning or an end, symbolise that our bond will last forever.

He whispered to me slowly, "I love you."

I did shy away from saying that in front of the priest.

Just when we came out of the Chapel holding hands, the usual hullabaloo of my relatives started, it was a task to collect them all and head our way back to the villa for lunch and rest of the ceremonies. He didn't let go of my hand the entire way, I could feel his sweaty palms in mine but this jittery feeling that I am going to be with him from now and forever gave me butterflies. I wanted to kiss him, seriously I could only think about this, but there were three other people in our car.

Punjabi weddings mean lots of drinks and starters, seeing my drunk uncles dance to punjabi tunes and my aunties prepping their blingy outfits for the next day kept us busy and away from the thoughts of being left alone in a room because technically our Hindu wedding was still to take place and we wouldn't be allowed to stay close to each other, not even sit in the same room. My uncles made sure they occupied his time and kept him away from wanting to see me.

Avanti went to and fro from our rooms to check what was happening and passing on our sweet little messages, she also clicked pictures of Nick having a drink with my uncles and showed them to me. Her mom had arranged a nice beige sherwani for him and a blush pink saafa which would match my outfit.

I was awestruck when my wedding trousseau arrived in a big wooden truck having the label of one of the most posh boutiques in Goa. On the canvas of white, it had kashida embroidery in blush pink colour covering most of the lehenga and an intricate golden zari border to complete that bridal look. A blush pink blouse with a deep back and a light red duppatta as my odhani. My mom gave her wedding jewellery to me, a polki necklace, her gold bangles mixed with chooda which is mandatory for us to wear and a maang tikka. My photographer friend from the magazine company I interned, volunteered to do a free photo shoot for us. He captured every little detail from the lehenga to me wearing those choodas, heels and maang tikka. Avanti suggested we do a messy bun letting some strands loose on my face with white roses decorating my hair.

I still couldn't believe that we are doing a second round of marriage and here I haven't seen him since yesterday. I was craving to see just a glimpse of him when my photographer friend Kartik, suggested we do couple pictures before the ceremony because we still have sunlight but later all the pictures would come out in dark and he wanted to bless the pictures with natural light.

They took me to the terrace garden of that villa where he was already waiting for me. God, in that beige sherwani and pink saafa he looked like those grooms on wedding magazines, standing with his palms joined in front of his face, he gasped when he saw me in this attire for the first time. I think I saw him well up a bit but then he wiped the creases of his eyes and smiled, that smile; the smile which could melt any hearts, the smile which said a hundred things about how much thrilled he was to have me as his wife.

I went and stood in front of him to hear some sort of appreciation for all the hard work that has gone behind creating this masterpiece.

"Aish… I, I have no words. You are looking like a fairy tale princess. Wow. I mean just wow, I am literally thanking all the gods that you are mine now." He held both my hands and kissed them, "I am going head over heels for you right now babe." I had to nod him a bit to make him realise everyone was watching us.

"Isn't she looking exquisitely gorgeous, like those vintage brides," Kartik was already taking our pictures after he said this to him.

Nick inched towards me and whispered in my ears, "tell him to stop complimenting you or I will break his camera."

"My god Nick, if you will break his camera how will we have precious memories to last our lifetime, don't you want to show these beauties to our children and grand children." I giggled covering my face carefully not to ruin the matte lipstick on me.

Maybe this possessiveness did the magic but we had terrific couple pictures that could ever come out, Kartik did a candid long range photo shoot where he was far away from us and asked to just talk naturally, just like we are always with each other; occasionally touching my waist and making me swirl. Every touch of his would send shivers down my spine, I just can't wait for everyone to leave us alone.

It was time for our Pheras, Panditji was all set with his havan kund for us to tie the knot, all the punjabi clan was full on excited in their glittery avatar; cheering and hooting at our arrival, flowers pouring in from every nook and corner. My cousins didn't knew of a subtle way to do this so they had pre installed the fireworks and once we started our Pheras, they didn't stop for the next hour. Panditji was explaining the meaning of each Phera and Nick held my hand tighter with each one. I knew he was listening to them very carefully unlike me who started feeling hungry and tired with all the wedding ensemble

We took the seven vows keeping the holy pyre as the witness, seven rounds or the Saptapadi for seven births to come, we promised to be with each other for eternity.

CHAPTER 7

Soon it was our wedding night or it should have been but then destiny had other plans for us, our Panditji advised my mom that we shouldn't be allowed to consummate our marriage that very night because there was some kind of pooja left which would be done in the wee hours of the morning, only then our lives would be blessed from above.

We were again taken to different rooms even after being a man and wife, I had no appetite of any sorts left; thoughts of embracing and kissing him haunted me, so my paternal and maternal cousins took upon them to divert my mind and started irritating and questioning me again and again that where are we going for our honeymoon, I sat down with my planner to tell them everything that I had decided for my honeymoon. Avanti brought in as many starters she could and pushed them through my mouth so that I still have energy to get up at 4 in the morning for the next round of pooja.

We never wanted to book a hotel or a resort, it's too formal; you always have to watch out how you dress up or speak or behave and this is our honeymoon; I wanted to be left alone, wild and unrestricted. I was going on the trip of my life time with the person I love the most; we were just married and I wanted to get away from everyone, i wanted to be one with him. I had done my research well and decided to book a villa which was way cheaper than resorts and would give us full privacy.

After binge watching tons of Korean dramas and romantic shows, all I wanted was the most perfectly romantic and intimate honeymoon whose memories would live young for years to come and stories which I may or may not glorify about.

The Serene villa was an absolute gem hidden perfectly in the valley covered with pine forests near Mashobra in Himachal.

Everyone wanted to put their ones and twos in deciding our destination but I knew I have to go somewhere in the mountains. I have seen beaches all my life but what intrigued me was the beauty of mountains, their calmness, the huge lush green peaks, the pesky narrow roads leading up to the snowy white tops. I had never been to any mountain city and I had told this to him as well, he had left the choice on me and all my family could come up with was Shimla and Manali saying even my mom dad went there for honeymoon but I knew Shimla and Manali are too much mainstream and touristy; I wanted something isolated. So instead of zeroing in on the city; I started looking for different properties online. I searched for houses on rent, Villas on nightly rent, camps, wooden chalets which are famous in that region. After straining my eyes over hundred options; stumbled upon a beautiful villa which instantly grabbed my attention.

It was like what I was thinking came out as a search result, everything that I needed to capture in the picture perfect honeymoon was right there in front of my eyes like God put that villa on my table. I instantly checked every detail on it, read every review, grasped the last information available on that villa. It wasn't that expensive and was fitting in our budget. We might need to cut short a night but that's okay.

The location wasn't in Shimla, it was near Mashobra, some thirty kms upwards that meant all the privacy we could get and the city also wasn't far if we wanted to visit. I didn't show him it's pictures, wanted to surprise him. I had saved all the money I got from my job and it could get us five nights of that Villa but I was over the moon when I told him that my wedding gift for him is our honeymoon. He was all ears about the plan and enthralled that I had laid out such minuscule details as if we were going on a mission; occasionally he grinned and I could see it from the corner of my eyes.

Nicholas was unlike other men who would take it upon their ego that providing for wedding and honeymoon is a man's business; his dad didn't leave much savings, he plummeted in life and everything else after Nick's mother died; as if he lost the will to live. All he had was the house we would now be living in and just his stipend that he got from the government; I knew everything in and out, hence I made sure that Nick should no where feel that he could provide less for me. I am going to build his empire, be with him till the very end. He was still to start his duty and before that he had one month, his line of command and position would soon arrive and we wanted to celebrate this one month as much as we could. It appalled me that after one month he'll be posted somewhere far away from me, again creating the distance between us.

I decided we should leave for our honeymoon the very next day of our wedding; otherwise my family wouldn't give us moment of solace. I had booked the flights from Goa to Chandigarh and then we would be taking a cab all the way to Mashobra enjoying the scenic route which I craved for. I had already pre booked the cab as well so we don't have to waste any more time at the airport.

During the early morning pooja, both of us were yawning, even he didn't sleep for a minute, "baba I hope this is the end of all ceremonies, itna to me military training me bhi nhi thaka," and he yawned again; seeing him I had to cover my mouth.

Soon after the rituals got over, we packed our bags and left for the airport. Going away from this and finally being able to sit close to him in the backseat and holding hands felt like a fresh wave.

"Are you excited to see the place I have booked," I asked looking into his eyes making circles with my nails in his palm.

"I am excited to be with you there, the place doesn't matters babe, no wife, I should call you wifey na," he took his palm up to kiss my fingers.

"Issshh, don't do it here, cabvala knows papa," I retracted my hand.

"So what, we are married now, we are legal to do anything," he grabbed both my hands now and held them tightly so I cant get back.

"Ya I know, but sab yahi kar loge?"

We both grinned and shied away knowing what was coming for us.

Dressed in a low waist skin tight denims and a pink crop top wearing mangalsutra, sindoor and chooda; I was looking like the perfect Indian bride going on her honeymoon. He was constantly teasing me that my attire and jewellery don't match, so I should change either of them.

"Heck, who cares, I am happy, you are happy, I don't give a fuck about anyone," I muttered all the way while collecting boarding passes.

"Aish, you've started cursing way too much, this journalism job has seriously made you a snob," he cut through my way to collect his own.

"I just used a single word, why would you comment on my job, you wanted me to take up literature and do what I like and now if it does have some side effects, you are brooding." I looked away.

"So would you be okay if I also curse in front of you occasionally?"

"Ya, I am totally okay with you cursing, we would be living together 24/7, there would be times when you would want to curse." My tone got a pitch higher.

"Why are you bawling? Everyone around is looking at us." We were standing in the security check queue.

"Oh so we are already fighting like an old couple, Nick we've been married for like 24 hours." The brawl got a temporary pause when we separated for security checks.

While he was collecting his watch and belt from the security trays, I picked up my hand luggage and walked fast ahead of him towards the boarding gate.

He called for my name but I didn't stop, how could we be fighting the next day of our marriage, the first day of our honeymoon, it should have been all lovey dovey and I was sulking.

I felt a tight grip of fingers on my left wrist just when I reached the departure gate, he pulled me back swiftly with one hand and I got off guard loosing my balance in the flip flops I was wearing. He held my bare waist with his other hand, "Nick"

"Shhh" he placed a peck on my lips to stop me from speaking any further.

People waiting for departure laughed at us thinking that a restless honeymoon couple couldn't wait enough to get to their hotel room.

I started blushing, all the blood raced up to my cheeks and I had to bury my face behind his broad shoulders to hide my embarrassment.

I couldn't look up to meet anyone's eyes till the time I reached my seat in the flight. Thank god the aisle seat of our row was empty. I looked out of the window, it was all sunny and humid here, god knows what weather is waiting for us there. We didn't argue after that little public display of affection. All through the flight, we were quite. Nick got some sleep but I was watching the clouds pass by holding his hand and occasionally looking at my sleeping husband's face. So innocent, that warm child like sleep.

Without any turbulence, in the flight and as well between us; we reached Chandigarh by noon and from there it was a 4 hour drive to reach our villa. The taxi that I had pre booked was waiting for us at the exit gate. The driver, Mr Gurinder was a jolly fellow in his mid fifties. He welcomed us, shoved our luggage in the little boot space and became a tour guide to us for the complete ride knowing that it is our first time in Himachal. He named every village or tourist spot that we passed, I still remember the route, Chandigarh-kalka-kasauli-solan-Shimla-Mashobra. He offered that if we want cab services for the five days we are staying there, but deep down we knew that we aren't going to step out. So we politely declined.

I can't describe in words what a beauty that route is. It is rightly called the dream destination of every nature lover, watching those plunging valleys covered with dense lush green forests of pine, deodar, oak and cedar is a treat to your eyes. It soothes your soul, its scenic grandeur views of gushing streams here and there and little waterfalls are so magnificent. In the month of may, evening air wasn't chilly but a pleasant cold. By the time we reached Mashobra;

It was already night and we had to turn on the GPS to find the exact location of Serena villa because the driver knew the famous hotels and this villa was kind of offbeat; secluded somewhere away from the city. We were guiding Gurinderji to take which left right and in night, its very risky to navigate the narrow roads in such hilly terrains and that too when it had rained. Somehow we contacted the owner and asked him to guide us and reached the villa before dinner.

The villa was a little five minute walk from the main road which was the only parking, then you have to climb a flight of stairs on a rough patch of mud and grass which was slippery due to rains. Now I was having second thoughts about booking this place as to what would be the arrangements inside. He understood my perplexity and held me from the back to push me walk up those stairs. But this moment of confusion was only for those five minutes, once we entered the villa; we forgot everything even the whole day's journey to reach here.

The villa was built in a historian theme with rustic wooden charm, paired with earthen colour palette. Britishers used to stay here, their were photos of officers and commanders staying there hooked up on the big wall of the living area, a teal blue lounger next to a giant wooden fireplace and the room was fitted with grey coloured carpets so you could walk barefoot.

The caretaker Raju; a boy in his early teens led us the way to the dining hall. The dinner was cooked by him already waiting to be served, it was simple but tasty and we were damn hungry so ate our way to the last bite. He wanted to show us around the property but we insisted to do it in the morning. He led us to the bedroom.

On the first floor of the villa, the bedroom had a wooden flooring and a mid rise four poster king sized bed covered with milky white net curtains and peach color bed-sheet with a matching comforter. Even in the month of may, nights were chilly. Big glass windows looking out to the valley, there was no TV or WiFi. This place was meant to be a buster from the chaotic life of cities, so it disconnected you from anyone or anywhere.

"I am going to take a shower," I took dibs on the washroom and he smiled; nodding his head and sat on the window seat which was a comfy bench type sitting laid with big pillows and little planters on the window pane; he was trying to look for a view but the night had spread its darkness.

The marble fitted bathroom with a walk in shower and even a fitted bath-tub, dresser attached; it was bigger than whole of my room and terrace combined. I turned on the hot shower to ease out the strain of the whole day. I changed into the pink satin bathrobe that Avanti was so determined in buying for me, she bought the complete honeymoon nightwear while constantly teasing me of wearing these in front of him, I couldn't even look at those flimsy under-wears and lacy thongs, those bras were just for the namesake, everything was visible through it so I decided to wear the bathrobe over those intimate clothings instead.

I stepped out of the shower and sat on the window seat near him, he was still absorbed by the pitch black darkness, all my honeymoon look was going unnoticed and I felt a little restless. How could he be sitting so calmly, his breath was normal while I was already breathing heavily. I got up to bring my hair ties, my hair was a little wet from the shower so I thought I should tie it up, just then he turned around to look at me and stopped me from going, held me from my waist and pulled back to sit on his lap. With a thud I was placed on his thighs, my wet hair sticking to his face, his jeans felt rough under my thighs and the satin bathrobe was slipping over my legs. I sat facing him with my hands on his shoulders held for support, he met me in the eyes, removed my hair from between us, gazed from my face to the buttery soft fabric that was half open on my thighs.

"God, you're so gorgeous, but you didn't have to go through this mile for me."

"Shhhh," I placed the tip of my finger on his lips and took him in my em-brace. I hugged him tight with my fingers clenched at his back. He grabbed me from my thighs on both sides of his waist and pinned me down on the tiny blue couch in one swift move, it didn't even take an effort on his rock solid arms. I felt his body weight on mine, I was breathing so heavily that he had to calm down my nerves before even kissing me. He just kept looking at my face and I could feel his hot breaths on my neck, I wanted him to come and dig into my neck, lick it, kiss it, bite it, suck it; do whatever he wanted, at least do something but all he did was to tease me by just staring at me. I tried to pull him close by clenching on his collar but he resisted to lay down on me. That was enough for me, I couldn't wait more so i arched up my back and took his lips into mine. I bit them hard for teasing me, I held my palms tight on the back of his neck to stop him from moving. It was our moment, it was meant for us only, so that we can unite and become one, forgetting our past or future, just living this with each other. He held my head from slipping back and kissed me with more intensity than I did. He sucked on my lower lip and than upper lip and back to the lower lip, he wanted to take his own sweet time exploring my lips, my mouth, he sucked on my tongue with his fingers rubbing on my neck and plunging to my cleavage. For a second he left the kiss and took a view of my cleavage and god knows what happened, he got up from the couch and took me in his arms and pushed me on the bed, it made a squeaky sound on the wooden flooring. We had to stop to laugh at the weird noise the bed made, water droplets from my hair were dripping on the bedsheet, he kissed the wet skin on my neck, I trembled with the heated kiss, beneath it was cold and on me it was burning fire. He licked the hollow gap between my neck and shoulders and remained there for a while leaving marks of his passionate love on me. The pit in my stomach was burning for more, to be absorbed by him, I pulled his T-shirt up and my handsome husband with that great Greek body was there, with all that tanned skin and abs; all mine. I touched every inch on his skin, bit him on his chest, left my nail marks on his forearms. I was trying to undo the button of his jeans, God; why is it so difficult, I tried but failed. He smiled seeing my uncounted failed attempts in opening his denims. He got up from the bed and undid his jeans, he hovered on me and removed the bathrobe. Those flashy red bra on my white wet skin was like a trigger for him. He took one of the straps in his mouth and slowly removed it with his teeth while licking my skin everywhere until he un hooked my bra. The bra was gone, I spread my legs for him to settle in my space, wanting his manliness to drown upon me. He slowed down to remove my panties, teasing me with his fingers on the wet part of my panties, it slipped down on its own leaving nothing between us but just the bare bodies, the love, the need, the passion, the fire burning within us. He inched down on me and sucked on my chin whispering how much he loved me and wanted me. With his body weight on mine leaving not a spec of air between, he touched my clitoris with his fingers, it was ecstatic. I wanted him inside me so badly, I digged my nails in his shoulders, he was rock hard and I was wildly wet that it went inside without any difficulty, I shouted his name with the initial pain I had but this ache of making love to him was so overpowering that I didn't wanted him to stop, after a while he realised we were doing it without the condom so he pulled out.

"God, why'd you stop?" I held his hand.

"Aish, wait let me wear the condom." He was frantically searching for one in his bag with one hand.

"Oh god, let it be, its safe time of the month," I was pulling him back on me.

"No, babe, this is too risky, wait, I'll wear it, I just can't find it." He was looking tensed now.

"Shh, I am telling you na, nothing will happen, I have my periods in next 4-5 days, so it's very safe, I wont get pregnant, don't worry, just come back na already." I wouldn't let him wait for a second, pulled him back and this time pushed him on the pillow and climbed on him, sat on his thighs facing him while he cupped my tender breasts in his palms pinching the erect nipples, I mounted on him and my long hair bouncing back and forth with the rhythm of our love making, I got tired soon so he took over and started doing the thrusts, our bodies were girating in rhythm. My moaning was loud enough to reach the ground floor and the bed noise was adding to it. I licked him on his earlobe and he couldn't control his orgasm, he came inside me, we both shuddered at the same time.

Breathless, I slept on his chest, tears of happiness flowing through my eyes and dripping on his chest making lines, he kissed my forehead, my hairs, he caressed me all through the night, holding me in his arms. In the little chilly weather under the soft fabric of comforters, we had united, we became one, I felt like the most luckiest and happiest person on this earth.

The morning sun and the mountain birds chirping waked us up, the first thing I saw was the calm and happy face of my love, sleeping with a baby face, I could see marks all over his chest and shoulders. Damn I must have hurted him bad last night.

I got up and looked under the bed to find my bathrobe but before I could wear it, he pulled me back, "Good morning Mrs captain, where are you planning to go?" He kissed me bare back.

"Ishh, Nick, let me get the bathrobe," I was getting sheepishly pink.

"No clothes, just you and me, last night you were in so much of hurry, I couldn't even look at you properly; let me devour my wife with my eyes at least." He laughed knowing that I would be embarrassed to talk about last night.

We were wrapped in the white bedsheet and the view of the valley was mesmerising. One can spend an eternity like this without even knowing. I was happy I made the right choice, "you liked this place na?" I looked back at him.

"It's okay, not that great as I was expecting," he said very bluntly.

"Sorry, come again, what? You didn't like this villa?" I was shocked to hear such a thing.

He snickered dramatically and I knew it was his way of teasing me, he just loved to play words with me purposely making me angry.

"Oh baby, I love it, there can never be a better place than this, my happy abode is you, wherever you are, that's the spot I want to be and oh yes that spot too," he touched me inside my thighs, "its so warm and amazing."

We cuddled and the cuddle led to another session of morning sex, we didn't care about the time or food, to satiate the hunger of the bodies was the priority.

"I want to savour every moment with you baby," he caressed my lips with his thumb; there were beads of sweat on his forehead. All the cold couldn't stop us from being naked throughout the day.

Somewhere in the afternoon we washed up and dressed up nicely stepped out of our room, the helper guy was ready with the lunch served on the table. We couldn't look him in the eye knowing he must have heard all those noises last night, we quietly ate our food and walked out of the villa for a walk.

The weather was charming, cool and cloudy, smell of the local herbs and flowers filling up the mountain valley, little shops selling maggi and tea were crowded upon and mostly they were honeymooners like us. I held his hand tight and walked slowly. The steep turns of the streets and the little sunlight left was sparkling on the tops of mountains making them look honey clad. Someone could capture this and put a postcard for a swoon worthy landscape painting. We were going down the alley so it was big steps pushing us forward with gravity and I was having this funny pain in my stomach holding me back to walk briskly.

"Babe are you alright? Is it hurting you? Your abdomen, is it paining?" He touched the zipper part of my jeans making sure I was okay.

"Ya ya, I am okay, its just grumbling, maybe I am still hungry and we definitely had too much of sex being it the first time, so its gonna hurt for a while."

"You were the one turning me on and wearing all those sexy, showy lingerie," he pointed at my cleavage.

"Isshh, shut up nick," I pushed away his finger and he snatched my hand to intertwine his fingers with it.

"You look so pink, like you're a teenager having your first kiss," he pulled on my cheeks which were cold.

"My first, second, hundredth and the last will be with you, my darling husband, my Mr captain. Arasso?"

"Arasso"

"Sarangae oppa," I looked up at him adorably and he frowned not knowing the meaning of this, "it's I love you in Korean buddhu."

We mingled with the cacophony of the market and rummaged through some shops for magnets and souvenirs. I always pictured a fridge in my house that would be covered with magnets from all over the world, from all the places I have travelled to; my magnets would be telling hundreds of untold stories about me.

"Let's go, have that kulhad chai," he sensed my uneasiness in walking.

I spotted a nice little cozy sit-out café, the untouched nature and the idyllic locale with occasional apple trees sitting here and there and a hot kulhad chai in your hand. I don't think people with fat bank balances can ever enjoy a moment like this.

This place was like a detox, come here leaving all your worries, baggage and phones. We bought some cream rolls and chips from a British bakery to binge in the night back at the villa.

It's always farcical how we become totally different persons while being on a holiday, we tend to forget how usually we behave in our routine mundane lives.

I asked him to buy a packet of condoms because he couldn't find the one he brought with him, "we can't be risking it for the rest of our days here mr." I gave him a sharp eye.

I don't know how fast days passed by, it was like setting up an alarm at 3 am to wake up at 5 am, before we even blinked an eye; our honeymoon was over, though we didn't do much, we mostly stayed in the villa occasionally stepping outside to buy something or to eat at new cafes. This was the space we needed to know each other's lifestyle, habits and just everything. We bathed together, even brushed our teeth together which he thought is gross but still I forced him to fulfill my whims and wishes. On the day of our return flight, we packed a slovenly room in our trunks. Everything was booked, our cab was waiting outside but we didn't wanted to leave. I wished we could stay a tad longer. My husband and I will begin the actual journey of marriage now, the duties, responsibilities, careers, our bonding with everyday highs and lows. I just embraced this calm; lying on his shoulder waiting for the storms that were about to show up soon.

We reached Goa, he had to join soon for his posting in East so all I did was pack his stuff, I had to buy new furniture also for our home, he dropped everything on me to suit according to my taste. He departed for Guwahati, and I was left alone with the poorly shaped house and oddly newly married cum housewife version of me. I did not see him off, saying goodbyes are the worst, I can never say this to my Mr captain; never. He knew I would be feeling low, so he called Avanti over and left just after she made herself comfortable in the house. I was swamped with to-do things and in this frenzy of events I had forgotten to keep a track of my periods.

And voila!

I was running late on my periods by almost 10 days. I thought its some stress issue or that I was sad after he went away.

"Babe, do you think I am bloating?" I asked Avanti, watching myself in the long bordered mirror which we just bought from a thrift store yesterday along with a small chequered coffee table and two wing chairs in teal blue color. I wanted to put up a hammock because that was the most trendiest thing that time in Goa but it was a bit expensive and nick asked me to defer for sometime. He was a self made man, though he never stopped me from taking any money from my parents but he particularly told me to wait to refurbish our house till the time his salary starts being credited.

"No , you're perfectly fine. What happened?" She said chewing on the warm sweet potatoes, Nick loved them.

"I am running late on periods," I mumbled to myself biting my lower lip.

Somehow she heard it, "wait, what?" She spat pieces of sweet potato. Wiping her mouth; she cooped up around me eying me suspiciously, "did you not use condoms?" She was rocking her head left to right in detestation.

"I.. umm. We did.. most of the time," I murmured again looking down on my toes.

"Tch tch, most? How can you be so careless? Did you do the pregnancy test?"

"No, why would I do the test, I am sure, I cant be pregnant, God, am I pregnant? Fuck!" I exhaled.

"No, don't fuck, you have already done it that too without protection, great. Let's go buy you a pregnancy test kit now." She grabbed her bag with so much of enthusiasm as if she already knew the result.

I was dismayed, I didn't wanted to be pregnant right now; my life had just started and I was about to rejoin my magazine company as a senior writer and blogger. I had no time to raise a child and I was just 22, it wasn't the correct age to become a mother, I hardly knew anything about it.

But that ship had sailed.

The test came positive.

I did a round two just to confirm and there it was, all my stupid biological sense in front of me, laughing his ass off; punching me in the face.

Why the hell did I tell him, it was a safe time and it was okay to not use a condom and what will I even tell him, he might have just settled in his new posting; how will I even say, Nick you're going to be a dad at twenty two.

Those words only gave me a thunder shock, I shivered from inside. Hardly fifteen days of our married life and how can we afford this stupidity. My mom and dad will kill me. And apart from that child bearing is no joke, I have a full fledged career in front of me.

The kind of news that always brings happiness and good luck was nause-ating to me. I sat down on the bathroom floor and covered my face, I let out a shriek.

Avanti was sitting outside the door and hear me scream, she banged on the door, "hey you, come outside, like right now; I am worried as fuck dude," she kept. on banging until I turned the knob.

I came outside holding both the positive tests in my hands. "Fuck, am I going to be a maasi soon?" Her laughter died and the upward crest turned downwards. Seeing my disheartened face, she questioned my ex-pressions, "are you not happy, if its making you this much sad, we can go and abort it today; there wont be any need of telling your mom or nick." I hugged her, held her tightly, she was continually patting my head em-phasising on the fact that its no big deal. But I knew it is a big deal; it was going to be a big deal for Nick, he would never want me to abort our baby.

Avanti only had the courage to disclose this to my mom, she stormed in-side our house shouting and throwing mellow drama like how did I even had the audacity of hiding something this big from her and why the hell was I having second thoughts about having this baby.

"Look beta, I had you when I was 20, so it is a perfect age, don't worry about what others will think; your family is there by your side, Nick is there, Avanti is there; who else do you want and soon you'll have a cute little baby in your arms who is going to look just like me." And that made me laugh, "no, mummy, I don't want one more punjabi maa, I cant handle two nagging people in my life." Just the thought of my baby having my mother's face made me burst into a laughter filled with tears. "Maa you think Nick would feel good about this? He's just joined."

"Every father has hiccups when they discover they are going to become fathers, men are not wired to adapt to every emotional and physical change easily but we women do."

"And you are strong betaji, I have raised you to be one of the strongest girls," she kissed my forehead. "You will yourself announce this to him, and do it today." She went back to her house to prepare something for us.

How weird this is; just some days back that was my house too; but now that's her house and this one's mine.

When he called me in the evening, I just wanted this to be out of my system, so I hinted him that there's something very important that he should know and when he literally begged to say what was on my mind, I gulped down my hesitance and whispered, "you're going to be a father," my throat choked at that.

"What?" His voice seemed a bit confused.

"You're going to be a father," I reiterated the fact.

"What?"

I checked the signal of my phone thinking I might not be audible enough but there was full network.

So this time I shouted in the speaker of the phone, "I am pregnant, can't you hear it?"

"I heard it the very first time"

"So are you speechless or just unhappy about this?" I emphasised on the unhappy word.

"No, no, stupid; why would I be unhappy. I am just processing what you said, like is it possible? isn't it too early like are you sure because we used condoms." So he was definitely left speechless.

"We did but not for the first time"

"But you said it was a safe time, didn't you?"

"Yeah so I was wrong, is there any problem with that? You can tell me up front that you don't want a baby right now," my voice was turning into cold anger now.

"Baby, why would I not want something that is a part of you and me. Okay first calm dow, who is near you right now?"

"Avanti"

"Let me talk to her" I passed the phone to her. She went out and was on the call for a very long time and it was sickening to sit there anticipating what they are talking about.

She later handed me the phone, "lets talk later," I didn't wanted us to fight over this.

"No, wait, listen to me very carefully Aisha, there cannot be a more satisfying news than this to my ears, I was unclear about the actual situation. You complete me baby and now you have completed us. This day is going to mark the history in our lives baby and don't you worry; I will come there as soon as possible. You don't have to be alone through all this."

"No, this is what I didn't wanted; you don't have to come back. You have joined just now and I can take care of myself, I was afraid that you might not want to have the baby right now." I wasn't able to hold myself from welling up.

"Please don't cry na baby, you are mrs captain, my mrs captain; you are far more strong than any one I know. We will sail through it smoothly without any bumps, I promise. And I am there na, just a few hundred kms away, one flight away from you."

We decided to visit a gynaecologist next day, Dr. Nirmala was the most familiar one to my mom, so she took me to her. At first impression; she might have thought that I am some young and reckless teen but she was a bit surprised after knowing that the wedding took place not even a month ago, though she calmed me down and made me understand what changes my body will go through now and owing to my less weight; she suggested I should start taking multi vitamins and I have to increase my diet as well. She wanted to do the first scan and told us to come a week later for a better scan.

On the way, I was googling everything on my phone from motherhood to pregnancy, I even ordered a book called 'what to expect' which had a five star rating on pregnancy books.

Every week went on like this, I used to read from the book; what changes should I be expecting, what should I eat, how should I workout and what organs of the baby are developing. My first scan came out normal, the foetus was growing and there wasn't any fetal distress seen or any abnormality.

He used to call me twice to confirm everything's fine and how my day went, what did the dr said or just to see the scan a thousand times over. Though at this stage, the baby was like lemon sized but he used to see the scan as if he can see the face or hands. "I am telling you it's a girl," he would say with resolute.

"I cant even figure out anything from this scan, its just a tiny little ball." I would laugh at his innocence.

Six months passed by, I was working full time with my magazine keeping myself super busy amidst morning sickness and pregnancy cravings, so that I don't have bad thoughts. Now I had a nice baby bump, with that people used to stare me at cafes and office meetings; even when I used to take the cabs. Mom never allowed me to leave the house without a kaala Dora and kaala tika on the back of my ear and she made sure I have more than enough to eat in my carry bags, that is why I was gaining weight rapidly. Seven months into pregnancy and it almost felt like nine months.

CHAPTER 8

I was sitting on the new swing that he had put up for me in the backyard of our house hanging from the old mango tree, it hardly bore any fruits now but its branches were rock strong. Nick had surprised me a month before my due delivery date. He had requested for a peace posting, owing to my maternity, he was granted a one year peace posting here only in Goa. I was contented that I wont have to deliver alone, though most of my pregnancy was over now but at least my husband is there with me at the most crucial time.

He was swinging me from the back but only a light push.

"You can push a little harder here Mr Captain; use those muscles even when you are on a leave." My peach dress was flaring with the air.

"No, not at all, I let you sit on a swing that is more than enough; I don't want both my girls to get hurt." He was smiling looking at my outgrown fully stretched thirty eight weeks pregnant belly. That meant I could deliver anytime soon.

I was still in awe with this amazing change that my body was undergoing. It was like a life changing event, like I was being reincarnated.

It is incredulous how much a human belly could stretch and be a centre of conception and create one new human being from it; sometimes two or even more. Amazing!

"How do you know it's a girl, you keep saying it's a girl it's a girl, how?" I looked back at him.

He came in front and knelt down keeping his palms on my belly, "because I want a baby girl."

"No I want a boy, just like you." I caressed his head.

"That you can have later, right now, we are having a girl for sure who has chocolate brown eyes just like you, long wavy hairs like you, silky soft skin and this exact baby face," he cupped my face between his hands. "Oh yes and your belly button, how did I forget this, I just love your belly button, it's the best thing in the world and I want our daughter to be exactly a copy of you." And he kissed my belly.

If there was bliss anywhere, it was here, with my man, with the father of my baby. All three of us in a picture perfect frame on a beautiful autumn evening on a swing with colourful leaves and flowers falling from above as the God himself was blessing us and whispering that this is the most surreal and enchanting feeling humans could possibly come across once in their lifetimes.

But at the same time, it's scary too, at a point in your life when you are too happy and fully absorbed with yourself you tend to forget that even this is temporary.

It was like eating a cake which was too sweet; that much sweet that once you finish it, everything else tastes sour.

That kind of feeling or premonition that when this happy phase will end; what will come next? That something will ruin it for you; call it negative energy or a sign of bad luck but something is following you.

Last few days of pregnancy were just the start of a phase which was going to be difficult. Days were uncomfortable but nights were dreadful, I had to get up pee every hour, it felt like I should put a mattress in the bathroom and just sleep there. There was too much pressure on the bladder plus the folic acid and iron supplements made me puke all the time. The taste of my mouth had gone sour and whatever I ate; it just didn't feel good.

Mom and Nick tried every possible way to make me eat healthy things but all I wanted to eat was chips. Nick was giving me all the time in the world he could give me except from his field timings; he had to go for his morning physical routine with trainees for 2 hours, then he would come back; have breakfast with me, and then he would leave by 10 and come back by evening.

When he wasn't there, mom dad would come over or I would go sit with them. This was like a benefit of having parents home and your marital home opposite to each other.

I well entered the last week of my pregnancy with 12 kg more weight than I weighed before pregnancy. I couldn't look myself in the mirror, I was swelled so much and sometimes I would cry that how am I going to lose this much and he would outrage me more by saying that I look better like this and there was no need of going back to previous shape; that way he would have to worry less.

31st August morning, I was painting the nursery we build in his dad's Room. We changed the bed and put up a white cot. I bought some cute wall stickers of Mickey and Minnie mouse in case. Mom took out her special soft rugs which she had bought from Kashmir. Those were expensive rugs which she never used and kept them in the trunk. Now she thought was a good time to dig them out.

 I wanted to paint the nursery with a neutral colour like beige or caramel but Nick insisted we do a light Pink going on his strong sense of future prediction that it's going to be a girl.

"Start from that upper corner," I was directing the boy who had come in to paint.

"You should go out and rest in your Room beta, I will get this done na," Mom had brought coconut water for me. She made me drink it every day saying that while she was pregnant she drank it every day and that's why I was born so fair and pretty.

"I don't feel like sitting maa, I am getting cramps if I sit down."

"Wait, what cramps?"

"Yeah just like I had in the initial few years of my periods but these are stronger," I was taking the support of the wall behind me.

"Since how long you are having cramps?" She started observing the end of my belly with her hands.

"I think they started last night"

"And you did not tell him about this"

"Then again he would have taken a day off, it could just be a false alarm and I didn't want to startle him."

"It's his baby as well na, what is the big deal in taking a day off. Look Aisha, I have sacrificed enough in my marriage while your dad was busy working and serving the country. I don't want you to live a life like me."

"But mom it would have been a waste taking a leave and then just coming back from the hospital."

"How are you so sure it's a false alarm just because you have read too many books on childbirth and parenting; you think you know more than 30 years of my experience." she was getting furious on me now.

"I am not sure if these are just cramps or contractions." I was getting restless now; my belly was enormous and heavy to be carried around like this and I was feeling suffocated and nauseas with the paint smell so I thought it's better to go out in the garden but then just my legs started to wobble. Mom took hold of me otherwise I would have fallen.

"I think you are having contractions not cramps dear." She made me sit on the sofa, "wait I'll call your dad, we should head to the hospital."

The pain was increasing now; mom and dad took me to the hospital and informed Nick on the way. He was there at the entrance of the emergency Room even before we had reached. He opened the gate of the car and took hold of my hand, "why would you not tell me; have you just lost it Aisha?"

"Why are you shouting, I am the one who's in pain."

"Sorry, sorry let's fight about this later; first let's get you inside."

He had already called for the wheelchair and the Nurse.

They took me in the maternity Ward, It was a shared Room but I was the only patient in labour that time. Mom, dad, Nick, all 3 of them were more nervous than me as if they were going to deliver the baby. They were looking at me as a parent looks at their children who are about to get their exam results.

The nurse changed me in a pink robe and asked to remove my under-garments, my engagement ring and the little moon pendant chain I was wearing in case there was need of a C-section. All 3 of them were waiting outside the Room and when they were allowed to come in I was lying in the bed and the nurse was taking my blood pressure, pulse and all other vitals.

I was hooked on oxytocin. I was getting contractions but they were mild and far apart so she increased the dosage to get me stronger and frequent contractions. Every time I would have a contraction; he would hold my hand and tell me to go easy and it kind of irritated me rather than helping.

When they started coming in after every 2 or 3 minutes; I started shout-ing to decrease the dosage as I was not able to handle the pain. They became stronger and stronger and I pierced my nails into his palms and shouted like anything.

"Calm down aisha, calm down. Breathe, breathe easy."

"Stop telling me to calm down. I am the one having a baby not you."

"OK relax and tell me what do you want to do"

"Call the doctor and tell her I can't bear this pain anymore, go, fast."

"Sure?"

"Go fast," I boomed on him.

"Ok I am going."

After a few minutes my gynaecologist appeared with him, "Good morn-ing Aisha, how are you feeling?"

"Not so good for me Doctor," I was groaning in pain.

"Relax dear, it's still a long way before you deliver," she pressed the lower end of my abdomen with her palms which was protruding at full capacity.

"Ouch…"

"Can you all please wait outside?"

"Why, what happened," Nick was alarmed.

"Nothing serious, I need to check how much the cervix is dilated."

My mom laughed at his horrified face and took hold of his hand to drag him outside the room.

She did a finger test on my vagina, "it's about 2-3 cms dilated, are you not having frequent contractions?" she removed her gloves.

"I am"

"Then it should have dilated more by now, let's wait for an hour more, I'll come back to check on you." She patted me on the head.

I couldn't do anything more than just lying, crying, and shouting in pain.

"Maa, I can't bear this, please, do something, maa," I was twisting and turning with acute pain.

"Aisha, relax, please, the doctor has told us to wait," Nick held me from getting up.

"One more time you say 'relax' and I will throw this on your face, come, you do this labour, come lie down on my bed," I held the vase on the bed stand.

"Aisha, behave," daddy looked up from his phone. God knows what he was doing on his phone all the time these days.

"Papa tell him no, why is he irritating me, It's already hurting so much."

"He is just trying to support you beta"

After waiting for quite a bit in total confusion and hustle as to what is happening, my gynae reappeared and demanded to do another finger test to check on the dilation progress.

"It's still the same even when we have induced you. Looks like you are going to be in labour for more hours than I expected, your progress is too slow and the cervix needs to be dilated more before we could start anything."

"But I can't bear more than this Dr. please, do something, I just can't, I am going to die like this," I literally begged in front of her.

"I have to consult your family first."

She went outside and everyone came in, demanding to know if I have asked for a C-section.

"Mom please, I can't wait more" I had big tears.

"Beta we can wait for some more time if we could have a normal delivery."

"Please everyone, why are you not believing me when I am saying I can't take it anymore than this, I am not brave like you Nick, I request you please, let her do the caesarean, please I beg you," I was at the verge of losing my calm and sanity.

"Okay okay Aish, we will do as you say, but Dr. is it safe if we go for the caesarean now?" all eyes were on her now looking for any signs of discomfort on her face.

"Yes it is, if she can't do this much labour, I doubt she'll be able to push in the later stage and her progress is extremely slow, the cervix is not dilating, for normal she has to wait for more hours and I don't think she would be able to do it looking at how she is reacting now." Her comment felt more as a taunt but I didn't care, all I wanted was to get the baby out as soon as possible.

Mom asked me, "are you sure you want to do the c-section?"

"Yes, please do it right away."

"Alright, I guess we have no other option left," the doctor instructed the nurse to wheel me into the operation theatre and to call the anaesthetist.

Nick kissed my forehead, "don't worry, you'll be fine, you are my wife, you are Mrs Captain. I love you; I am waiting here for both my girls."

The OT did look scary with a dozen flood lights on the ceiling and tools everywhere, they made me sit on the Operation table first and the anaesthetist who was a guy was already there, he asked me to sit straight and with a hard push injected epidural in my spinal cord, the injection did cause me some pain but then slowly numbness took over half my body, I couldn't feel anything below my chest. Its weird how you feel like a cow, sitting naked in front of people, someone is injecting you; other one is pushing on you, all this while they are seemed to be so normal and their usual banter felt as if it's no big deal.

They started the process; it was all foreign to me like the doctor giving some instructions to the nurse and the anaesthetist, I could hear metal tools clicking and noises outside the OT.

The doctor was talking to me while she was making a horizontal cut on my abdomen, I could see blood on her gloves, then she asked the nurse to push my abdomen, to push harder; I saw her hovering over my chest and abdomen and using her hands dramatically and suddenly there was silence, there was a squeaky little noise, then a faint cry and then a loud outburst of wailing and grunting.

Dr. Nirmala came to me; she was holding the baby upside down from the legs and to check how conscious I was; she asked me, "tell me, is it a girl or a boy?"

I was fully aware of the things surrounding me, I looked closely at the baby and with sheepishly crying voice I said, "Girl"

"Good girl, you have given birth to beautiful daughter," she smiled and went away to hand over the baby to the paediatrician sitting at the behind; ready to examine the baby like her weight, pulse, to remove extra water from her throat to and to clean the umbilical cut and cover the baby with warm clothes.

She came back and started the sutures on my belly; with every stitch she would direct the nurse to cut the ends. In half an hour my C- section was completed. While taking me out from the OT, it was a fuzzy feeling; I wasn't happy or sad, in pain or valour.

"Congratulations, you all have been blessed with a baby girl," she announced to my uneasy family waiting outside.

I heard Nick shouting, "I knew it, I had told her, it's a girl, she wouldn't believe me mom, I can't believe I am a father now." He must be ecstatic.

––––––––––––

My days were filled with tears and diapers and nights with breast milk and powder milk. I was dishevelled all the day and most parts of my body ached with after effects of a C- section. Your nipples are always sore, the heavy period flow is altogether uncomfortable, the abdominal pain is a nightmare, the stitches and the rashes make it unbearable to even sit or walk around, while lying down I felt like a whale; I couldn't even look at my body while bathing. The sleepless nights had given me dark circles and headaches. The excessive intake of ghee gave me heartburn and acidity.

The mixed feelings of a first time mom are weird, sometimes I felt ecstasy of delivering other times I was gloomy, I felt anxious that will I be a good mom; I felt frustrated that why do women have to go through this and cursed the entire male fraternity; I felt overwhelmed about what had happened but in the end when I looked at my little baby; at what I have given birth to, all I felt was peace.

It took me more than two months to come to my usual normal self, I started going out for walks while my mom took care of Anna. We named her 'Anna' because that was nick's mother's name. I started to take care of myself, my appearance and hair; I wanted to rejoin the company so for that I had to get back in shape. Nick helped me a lot during these tough times; he would get up in the middle of night to Anna wailing and crying; trying to calm her down and would let me catch up on some sleep. He would personally monitor my walking and yoga sessions and my diet. Whenever he would return from the cantonment area, he would scoop up Anna from the cradle and would swing her in his arms, sing to her, make silly faces and make her drink the feeder. Even when he got tired from his reporting duties and physical training hours, he never showed it on face, all he did was loved her and me unconditionally.

Men in uniform are supposed to be hard, strong and brave from outside. They hide their emotions inside a shell. But when he was around me or Anna, I saw the softest and kindest human being.

CHAPTER 9

My heart was sinking terribly, as if the whole ocean was trying to drown me, that feeling when you are in a very deep sleep and you are trying to swim hard to the shore; you are gasping for breath; you are pushing yourself towards the surface no matter how hard the waves hit on you but every time the water pulls you down more; all the efforts are going in vain and you can't see yourself surviving from this kind of situation and then you suddenly wake up, covered in sweat and heartbeat thumping fast; with trembling hands and legs.

Only this time it was no dream, it was reality all in front of me.

"Breaking News", the channel was blurting out loud. I don't remember the face of the journalist who was speaking, but she had that irritated look on her face like she was dragged in middle of the night from her slumber to report this incidence. She was telling the world about this incident, "Illegal child trafficking racket busted, and 13 adolescent girls were found drugged and half naked. The police went there on an inside tip and people nearby could hear gunshots for hours. Due to huge number of people involved; Army backup had to be called. The terrorists had huge supply of ammunition. The duel between army and the gang went over for more than 5 hours. The whole area has been seized and all the hotels and resorts in this area have been put to surveillance. Foreigners and other tourists have been asked to move to safer places from here."

That's it.

The blur night vision pictures started playing on the screen one by one in which some girls were being carried in an ambulance with their faces purposely blurred; there was fire everywhere near the old lighthouse in which they had sneaked in. journalists were leaping at every bit of information from the local police posted and the medical team which was present there. There were bodies being carried away, some injured; some dead. It was a dreadful scene.

She started repeating this piece with more calm face and instantly I wanted to smack her face down, I wanted to smack the bloody TV down. How the hell she could be so cold and calm, how the hell was it just another piece of news she was reiterating. The person in that backup team was my life, my whole freaking life, my love. How could they speak about it so casually but this is what they do right. Until and unless it affects us, we could have even changed the channel saying that the world is going to crap these days.

Nick had just mentioned it to me before leaving in the evening that it was a routine drill and they had to check some neighbourhood for illegal substances, it wasn't serious matter and he would return in few hours and that I should go to sleep without waiting for him. I didn't know what has actually happened, nobody knew. And I couldn't trust this Tv journalist so I had to look for myself.

I started calling the Headquarters. I called every number I had but there was no response. Some weren't picking up and the office boy who had picked up the landline had no clue as to what had really gone behind all this. I called his senior but he disconnected the phone telling me to keep calm and that I will soon be updated about things.

I called the families of his squad but they were equally clueless and asked me to call them if I hear any news about it.

I started weeping in front of the TV, hopeless and unable to do anything sitting from here and just waiting for the calls. My mom shut the TV because we were too miserable to watch it again and again. "Nothing bad has happened, why don't you go and sleep inside with her. If you get a call, I'll wake you up beta."

"How can I sleep maa, knowing that he went for this? His phone is off and I am unable to reach anyone." I was now crying hysterically.

"Why are you thinking anything bad, he might be busy saving all these injured people, he will call you as soon as he gets time," I knew she was just pretending to be brave in front of me but deep down she was afraid just like me.

"Your dad is calling his superiors to find out what happened, don't worry beta, I know God wouldn't do anything bad with us."

"I wish mom, I wish; that there is some God who might look up to us right now and would help us." It was difficult to think straight at this moment; all that was left was to join hands in unison to pray. Praying to Jesus or Guru Nanak, didn't matter, all mattered was that one soul above us could listen to our prayers right now.

Amidst all my crying and the phone calls, I heard Anna crying. I had forgotten to give her milk before sleeping. But I was in no condition to go and feed her so instead mom went inside with a bottle.

I just sat on the sofa. Blank.

I could hear mom singing to her "Satnaam satnaam satnaam ji, shri Waaheguru waaheguru waaheguru ji" while she was feeding her.

It soothed me as well for a moment, listening to her calm melodious voice.

Just when I was lost in her voice with my closed eyes and joined palms, my phone rang at 2:05 am; it was from the military hospital. They told me that Capt. Nicholas has been brought here and I should come quickly.

My dad came running from our house telling that Nicholas was fine and he was taken to the hospital. I told him, I got the call. Mom stayed with Anna and we rushed off in our car. I was wearing the cream colour pyjamas with tiny roses on it which Nick had bought me a few days back and he absolutely loved them. He couldn't stop bragging about himself that his choice was so great. He got similar ones for Anna in a smaller size. These days this was his usual lookout, he would buy the same thing in two sizes; one for me and one for Anna. He would be so satisfied looking at us in similar clothes, saying he has got the two most gorgeous women in the world.

I was looking outside the window and there were tears which I couldn't stop, dad was continuously asking me to stop crying as Nick was fine, nothing had happened to him. But did I trust the words coming out of his mouth, did I trust the situation, did I trust my destiny, my luck?

I was running helplessly inside the hospital reception floor asking for directions or whereabouts about him. The pungent smell of the floor cleaner was gut churning. Nurses were running in frenzy; somehow I held the elbow of one aged nurse.

"2:05 am"

"Sorry?"

"2:05 am"

"Can you hear me? Are you okay?"

"I got a call at 2:05 am saying my husband is here."

I was repeating my sentences in half circles and looking at the rust old blue watch on the corner of the wall spoiled by the cob webs.

"Yes, I understand, can you please have a seat," a nurse in mid-fifties was touching my shoulders.

"Where is my husband, I got a call at 2:05 am and I have rushed as fast as I could, my daughter is asleep at home, where the fuck is my husband," I clenched my teeth in anger and spewed every word at her.

"I really don't know you are talking about whom because we have a number of casualties right now and I am afraid I can't address your grievance at the moment but can you please calm down and sit," she was trying to soothe me but I was all the more getting agitated.

"My husband, Captain Nicholas Martin, he was brought here a few hours back, I got a call at 2:05 am and I had to call my mom to look after my sleeping daughter and I hurriedly drove here in my pyjamas and see I fall down on your stupid stairs, why can't you put a 'caution' sign; I have bruised my knee," I pointed towards my right knee which was now bleeding. "And all you can tell me is that you don't know where my husband is." I don't know what got into me, I wasn't rude like this but I was so fearful at that moment and bitter with this irresponsible attitude of the government hospital staff that I could have bit anyone who would have argued with me.

"Please sit down, let me call the doctor in charge, here drink this."

"Can you please check on my husband if he's fine," I sat down on a squeaky wooden bench.

"Yes I will check," she reassured and left me and my dad on the bench.

I don't know what was in the paper cup, water or something else because my hands were trembling and the liquid splashed on my knees stinging the bruise I got and with that I went blank….

I woke up on a hospital bed in a different stingy room. My head was pounding and some IV was running into my wrist. The vision was blurring but I could make out that my parents were discussing something with the doctor.

As soon as I tried to move, they came near to me; mom held my hand, "how are you feeling sweetie," she had cried a lot, I could differentiate her heavy gloomy voice.

"I….i .." I gasped for air.

"Maa listen," I choked. I felt a loss of words.

"Yes beta, tell me," she was holding me tightly and came close to me.

"Mom where is he… is he okay… where is he. Please tell me he is fine mom," I tried to speak while breathing heavily.

"and where is Anna, why are you both here?" I looked around the room for her.

"Avanti is with her at home, don't worry; she's fine." She assured me by tapping my palm.

"Nick is fine na maa? Please I want to see him, is he injured? Why is no one telling me anything? Dad, please at least you tell me, where is he?" I looked at him at the further corner of the room where he was standing.

He didn't move or say anything rather he just walked out of the room.

I pulled out my IV syringe with a jerk and shouted at the nurse standing nearby, "can I please see the doctor in charge here." I tried to stand up but I was feeling dizzy with the medication.

"You can't pull it out like that, you fainted in the night and your blood pressure dropped severely that is why you were hooked on Orvaten and IV fluids." she screamed at me.

I paid no heed to her and bolted towards the reception area, she ran behind me. I got dis balanced on the slippery floor which someone was cleaning and just then I saw Dr. Nirmala who did my C-section. She came towards me and held me up, "What is wrong with you Aisha, why are you creating a commotion since last night, tell me."

I started crying hysterically, "I am feeling so helpless Dr, why is no one taking me to Nick, where is he?" I put my hands on my face to hide the tears.

She held me from the back, "come with me."

We went into another doctor's office, "Good morning sir, she is the wife of Capt. Nicholas Martin," she made me sit in a cane chair.

"Oh, how are you doing now, I heard you fell on the stairs and fainted last night." He came to examine my eyes and the bruise on my knee.

"I am fine" and I wiped my nose.

"I will have to take you somewhere, can you come with us," he put down his coat and gloves on the table.

I slowly nodded.

We walked from his office to the elevator. The second floor had strong smell of alcohol and hospital cleaner and something else, I couldn't decipher.

I had dimmed vision as if walking in dreams, I was losing balance but my parents were their walking behind me and holding both my hands.

We stopped at the last cold iron slide door.

Mortuary

Why are we standing in front of a Mortuary?

I turned back to my mother, "maa what's wrong with you, why are we going to a mortuary. Can we please leave?" I turned to walk back but the doctor told me to come inside.

"I don't want to go in there, I'll puke because of this smell, and please I want to go out." I looked at him.

"There is something inside that you should see," he told me.

"There is nothing inside that I want to see." I removed my parents hands from my arms and shouted at them, "please take me to Nick, I request you all, why are you torturing me like this?"

They all forcibly dragged me inside. Any human being would cringe at that sight; it was the scariest place on earth.

Everyone was clinging on to me because I would run away.

We crossed tables with dead bodies covered in plastic sheets. I was mortified. I looked at my dad with a face on which questions were plastered, he didn't look back at me, just gripped me for support.

We stopped at a hospital bed in the rear end, it wasn't covered in plastic like others but a white cotton sheet drawn till the face.

I watched horror unfold in front of my eyes.

The doctor removed the sheet from the face.

There.

There he was.

My husband.

My love.

My life.

Lying there like idiots, not thinking about me, not fussing over Anna, not looking at me with those lovely eyes, not talking to me, not caressing my forehead, not pulling my cheeks until they turned blood red.

Captain Nicholas Martin

The bravest man I knew in my entire life was lying still on this rotten bed. Captain Nicholas Martin, Para commando, special forces, Indian Army.

I have never seen him sleep like that, straight with an expressionless face. His hands and legs were lying straight like a line drawn on paper. He would never sleep like that, he fought for space on the bed, slept like a baby, sometimes cuddling me and other times pushing me off the bed with his arms at ninety degrees. He slept with open palms and open mouth which I would close in the middle of the night after taking stupid pictures of him. His mouth was closed right now, lips weren't moving; nothing at all.

I touched his hand which was as cold as ice, I removed it instantly in fear that my demons would come to life. I wasn't ready to accept this. I touched his hand again, "Wake up, wake up Nick, come let's go, Anna is waiting for you at home, come."

There was no answer.

"Aisha.." mom looked at me, "he is no more Aisha."

"Ssshhh… mom, he is just pretending to sleep, he will get up if you all leave the room, go, go everyone, leave the room" I got loose from my parents grip.

"Aisha, look at me, he is not going to wake up, he martyred in that incident," the doctor jerked me from the shoulders.

"That's not possible, he had promised me, he will come back by morning and it's almost morning, he should be up any time soon, he always keeps his promises." I wanted to cry but the tears weren't coming.

They all took a step behind and the doctor told something to my parents when my mom started crying out loud.

"Mom why are you crying, he will be up soon, look at him, he's fine, he just needs to take some rest."

My mom hugged me and moaned on my shoulder, I didn't understand why she was crying so much. Suddenly then the smell inside hit me, I was feeling claustrophobic. It felt the room was closing down on me and I would be crashed inside with these dead bodies here forever, I ran outside gasping for some air and puked. The nurse standing there took hold of me and shouted for a stretcher, I was going to faint again in her arms.

Once again I found myself in the same room I woke up this morning, my clothes were changed and I was wearing an ill fitted hospital gown. I was mostly unconscious but still tears were rolling from the side of my eyes and the doctors said it's a good thing that I am crying, if not; I could go in a state of shock where I wouldn't register the truth ever. It could mentally harm me so it's better to cry it out.

I asked mom and dad if we could just go back home because this place was making me more sick and I was worried for Anna. Though Avanti was taking care, and she's been more than just a maasi to her but still, I haven't stayed away from her for this long ever.

There were two other of his squad members who were martyred saving the neighbourhood residents and the abducted girls. The workers of the hotels nearby, who had tipped off the police were also brought to the hospital to identify the bodies of the illegal immigrants. It was a filthy mess there and I didn't want to see it more for a second. I knew we would not be given Nicholas's body until the officials came and all this has been properly documented and medical reports signed. So there was no use sitting in this blood house, I wanted to see Anna as soon as possible.

Mourning is different for everyone. Some will cry their hearts out and let go of all the agony, some will hide the pain from others and bury the memories in their hearts to never let it go; that way they think, they can keep the person alive inside them. I was the second one; I didn't cry much, I was trying to hold myself up thorough all the last rites and rituals even when my aunts came bawling and shrieking on me. There weren't tears, there wasn't any feeling that he's not here; it felt like he's on a mission and will come back soon. His disappearance did not register on me; everybody said I am not coping well with this. Well how do you even cope up when the person around whom your life revolves melts in thin air; how do you imagine your remaining life to be?

The body was kept at the army cantonment area for honours. We went there along with Anna, she should see her father's face for the last time though she will never remember her father. His body was placed on a high stand with two other soldiers in the centre of the parade ground, big flames were lighted, all the senior and junior officers were standing in lines. Everybody paid there tributes to the martyrs, the government officials were first. Amid the chants of "Bharat Mata ki Jai" and "Vande Mataram", several people came forward to pay floral tributes to the three soldiers who achieved martyrdom. The families of other two soldiers were also there, bidding tearful adieu to there sons, husband, brother. The wreath laying ceremony happened with the personnel of Indian military and they saluted the bravery of these soldiers. Everybody was crying except me, I was only figuring out the face of my husband, did it change in one day, will he really not get up from there, maybe he will return after a year just like he did the last time.

The final salute and the procession began for the funeral, they neatly folded the Indian flag laid over his body and placed it in my open arms.

The Indian flag.

CHAPTER 10

People came and gave condolences to my family, I don't remember for how long it continued; I felt harassed every time someone touched my face or hugged me saying, "hamari phool si bacchi pe kesa pahaad toot pda", I wanted to run out of the house, walk all the way to the beach and sit there, alone; all alone. The atmosphere was choking, they tried hard to make me cry, showed me our wedding pictures or talked continuously about him; I didn't shed a single tear. Why should I cry, I knew he was going to come back like magic, like in all those Bollywood movies I have watched, all those Korean dramas I have seen; I knew someday he would reappear in front of me and we would laugh how he fooled everyone. I forgot that I have seen his dead body.

Slowly the relatives and friends emptied the house, I could finally breathe in my own space now. Several hours would elapse by looking out of the window, looking at the wall, the ceiling fan. Sometimes I would look at his cupboard, I still didn't had the courage to open it, his things, his clothes; everything was drenched in his smell. The Bible that he used read, it had a bookmark in it which I gifted him, if he would have come back, he would read it from the next page. His another pair of freshly washed and ironed uniform was hanging in the shelf with the name tag of 'Capt. Nicholas Martin'. The uniform that he wore for the last time was folded in a box and with several other belongings of him was handed over to us. For many weeks, I did not open that box; I didn't had the heart of opening it and seeing the blood stained uniform or those little things that he kept in his locker in his office building.

I cursed God.

I cursed everyone around me.

I cursed my daughter and I cursed myself.

I regret marrying him and getting pregnant and making him come here, had I not been pregnant; he wouldn't be here in that incident and he would be alive somewhere.

Why God why? Did I really do something bad in my previous life, why did you punish me so harshly. We just started our lives, did you really do this to me, Anna and him. Why did you got us married if you wanted to take him away, why did you gave me a daughter if you wanted to take her father away. Why are you so selfish, you took away nick's mother, father and now him. Did you want to reunite them up in heaven? I never got answers.

But one day a miracle happened, after almost a year of his martyrdom; life was getting normal. I started going to the office, I put Anna in a play school cum creche where she enjoyed her time with other kids, she hardly knew that her father was missing from her life. Sometimes I got jealous from her that she doesn't remembers anything about him.

Every time I got sad, she would come to me with a big smile with her tiny teeth showing and she would say something in a cute way with gibberish language that would vanish all my sorrows.

Mom dad and Avanti used to take turns to baby sit her while I was in office, three of them were my support system; my pillars, if not for them; I would have fallen long back.

Dad was now retired so he wanted to keep Anna most of the time, he would take her to school, parks, the same ice-cream shop we used to go. He would buy her a new toy every time they went out. She was happily being spoiled by her nana nani.

But my life, it never made sense to me until that day. It was a Sunday and

I had finally decided to clean up the house. I was sceptical to what I will find and will take me back to those horrid memories. I had already done away with my wedding outfits and pictures.

That day I opened the box.

It was covered in dust.

After cleaning it from outside, I spilled the stuff on my bed. I wasn't worried that Anna will roam around and touch all these things; she was with her nana.

I never knew what he kept in his locker, there was his wallet, his driving license, a few sports T-shirts, an extra pair of shoes and socks. There was a photograph; it was us. Me n him. We clicked that picture in Mashobra. How happily and madly we were into each other. The way he was holding me in that picture, you could see so much of love and content in his eyes. They were sparkling bright, the view behind was beautiful. I hugged that picture. I kissed him in that photograph.

Beneath all these, there was a folded paper, it had turned pale yellow with all the dirt. I pulled it out from all other things, I opened the creases of the folded paper, it was a letter.

A Letter.

A letter written by him, it was his handwriting. He never wrote me a letter. He never mentioned writing a letter. He didn't even write me anything for the time he left me for the training. What am I supposed to do with this letter now? Should I read it?

If he wanted me to read this letter; he would have himself given it to me.

I folded it back.

I opened it again, the dilemma of reading or not reading it was crossing my mind.

I threw it outside the window and looked away.

The next second I ran outside and scooped it up; cleaned it with my own dress, slapped myself and sat down to read it. It was the same paper from the handmade diary I gifted him. His handwriting was still as bad as it was in school.

My dear Aisha,

I find it very silly to write letters, like I can say everything to you in front of you so what's there to write in a letter. What do people write in love letters, I don't understand. But I wanted to write one for you, I don't know if I will ever give it to you maybe you will get to read it one day.

If I start comparing my life before you and after you, I cant thank god enough for letting me have you in my life. I think god gave you in recip-rocation of taking away my mom dad. Nevertheless I wanted to thank you that you accepted a broken person in your life, you healed me, you loved me, you taught me how to love and live, you taught me how to be positive. You never left me alone even when I made life tough for you by going away. We grew together Aish, i saw you becoming mature from that teenage girl, the way you talked, you smiled; everything froze for me. I can still close my eyes and picture us kissing on that beach, how gorgeous you looked. You helped me through the toughest time of my life, you took care of my dad when I wasn't around. I can never repay you or your family in anyway.

I wish someday I can fulfil your dream of taking you to South Korea. I wish I can earn that much and treat you to a really nice trip in South Korea and even if I cant afford it, I will sell the house and take you there; we can live with your parents. I have considered them my parents so we can all live together under one roof like one big happy family.

The day you said "yes" to marrying me, I felt the luckiest of all. You know I keep bragging about you in front of my batchmates, I have shown them your picture and they were rooting up for me that I have got the prettiest one of all. But above everything baby, your heart is so kind, so warm, I can die in that place and I can die for you. I will kill anyone who even thinks bad for you, I am afraid to loose you so you please need to take care of yourself love. Even the thought of you being hurt makes me clench my fist.

You are the bravest of all, you are far more brave than me, that's why I call you "mrs captain". So you will prove that you are a captain, you will fight, you will live a great life; you will become the best version of yourself and of course I am always there to stand beside you.

We will build a strong team, you and me will make the perfect life for us. I know we are going to make it in future, the kind of life you want, the kind of love that you deserve. I promise I will love you more than anyone can ever think of. You have placed your trust in me, you have given me the rest of your life so I will devote my everything to you. I am like an unsolved puzzle and you are that one missing piece who will complete me.

I am sorry for all the times I have been rude to you or did things without thinking how they will affect you. I will never make you upset or let you cry Aisha, more than me; you are my heart, blood and body. I now understand how my dad must have gone through when mom died, it must be horrifying to live alone and not being able to share anything with me.

I promise to always stick around, I promise to be healthy, I promise to become the best husband, I promise to prove myself a good son to your parents.

Even if I am far from you Aisha just remember one thing that I only want happiness for you. No matter where I am; ill always be able to see you, to hear you so you better not cry when I am away. All you need to do is close your eyes and you will find me running back to you, in your arms is my home.

I love you Mrs captain

First time in that year, I actually cried, I cried my heart out. I shouted; I pulled my hair; I dug my own nails in my palms. I clenched my lips because I was screaming with pain; all that pain that I hid came gushing out.

I burst into tears.

There was no date on the letter but I could decipher that it was written sometime after our marriage maybe when he went to the East but before my pregnancy news because no where he mentioned a child.

Had he known that this calamity was waiting for us, how could he have written things about him being away. Was he preparing me from future disasters. Why did he even write any of it making me crumble again, I felt like a child who's lost in a fair.

I got up and embraced myself as if he was hugging me with his letter, I let all my pain wash away in tears. I didn't wipe them; they needed to flow for me to bring back a smile on my face. He indeed made everything alright. He promised to be with me and here he was with me in the form of this paper.

I will not disgrace him by living like this.

Army men step forward for the security of their country when everyone steps back. I am his better half, I can at least take a half step forward.

If he's watching me from somewhere up, he wouldn't be proud of me. I will make him proud, I will not make him regret marrying a coward girl. He called me brave, I will live up to his expectations. He wants me to take care, he wants me to live a great life and so I will do. I looked up in the sky just like he did when he earned the Maroon Beret, "I love you Mr Captain and I will do as you want, you see here is your command and I will obey," I waved the paper in air.

I laughed

For the first time, I laughed; tied my hair up in a bun and got back to sorting the house, "I will sell it, I will live with my parents," I kept mumbling to myself while arranging card board boxes and filling them up with different things. I played my favourite music and opened his cupboard, hugged his shirts.

I was no more in remorse.

I announced my decision of selling the house and travelling to South Korea which was his wish in the letter, I showed it to my mom dad.

"It was his last wish, he wants me to go there."

Mom and dad looked at each other in confusion, they thought I am still not in my senses.

"I want to show him that I can still live happily with the memories he's given me, we will live together maa and we will raise Anna to be brave like him." I hugged her.

I had decided things I wanted to do, I will write a book.

A book about love; about me and him. But there was more to be written than just us, it will be the story of every Army wife. It will be a story of Army couples, their families, their children, their tragedies. The emptiness that is left behind the sacrifices made by our brave soldiers. They give their lives for the country but does the country give anything back to the bereaved. With what facilities and help are they left with. We already know how less the salary of soldiers are, their remuneration is less than a call centre employee; the one who is serving the country by risking his own life, sacrificing their family life, he is not paid sufficiently though they don't care about it. They don't join the Army for money, its all about love and patriotism for their nation, for the honour of serving.

I freshened up the next morning; dropped Anna to her play school and headed straight to my office. Seeing me storming around the office, my colleagues were happy that they got to see the old Aisha back. I knocked at the cabin of Sunita Ma'am.

"Good morning Aisha, its so good to see you. Have you been keeping well?"

"Yes Ma'am, actually I wanted to say something."

"Oh no Aisha, please don't leave the job, take as many leaves you want, work from home but don't leave the job." She was worried for me.

I smiled, "no ma'am, actually it's the opposite. I wanted to start working in full swing. I want to be productive around here."

"Ahh thank god, I was so tensed for you Aisha," she got up from her chair and came close to me, "you are like my daughter," she patted me.

"I want to write a book Ma'am, a book about my story and several other Army wives or mothers who have lost their sons, husband."

"That's a great pitch Aisha, I will make sure our company publishes it. Have you started working on the manuscript?" She had the same enthusiasm that I had in my voice.

"I will start today Ma'am, after the office hours I am going to meet some women and interview them."

"You don't have to sit here till evening, finish off your work here till lunch and then go start working for your book."

I couldn't thank her enough.

My first on the list was Mrs Vibha, I wont disclose surnames in my book owing to the safety and privacy of everyone in their families. I went to her house, it was a sweet little abode kept so clean and managed, I felt ashamed that how messy my own house was. She also had a son almost the same age as Anna, he was playing around with his little bike.

She was so accommodating, even when she felt uncomfortable while answering some of my questions, she never asked to discontinue the interview. She told me how scarce the medical facilities are in military hospitals when she needed treatment for her child. Where is the tax payers money going if not towards the betterment of services given to the nation's security.

For the next 6-7 weeks, I didn't sleep. It was like an adrenaline rush for me. Mornings went by prepping Anna for school and then office and then my book. I didn't stop writing until my book got completed.

The day I mailed my first draft to Sunita Ma'am; I called the property dealer home to sign the Sale agreement. The buyer had quoted a decent price, they were some foreigners who wanted to live in quite place in Goa away from the cacophony.

I signed the deed and got my cheque.

For the last time I glanced at the empty walls, I have already taken with myself every last bit of memory that house had. It was only a roof and walls now.

I bid farewell to this abode and welcomed my new life, Nick will always be there with me, I wasn't afraid anymore to look at his pictures or read that letter umpteenth time.

I had taken a one month leave to travel to South Korea and Sunita Ma'am had heartily agreed to it, she also paid for travel expenses. She wanted me to cover my travel in a blog and write articles for the magazine about an Indian solo girl travel to Korea. So it became a work cum holiday travel.

I never had to worry that who will take care of Anna, more than me, my mom was the actual mother to her. I had the privilege of my mom dad being with me but what about those who don't have their families support, think about the hardships those women must have faced in such situations.

I promised Anna to bring her the complete Hot wheels track set while coming back. She loved cars and robots more than dolls or kitchen sets. I made a mental list of things to buy from duty free.

I packed very light in a rug sack and just took the essentials, my camera, laptop, diaries, stationary, one jacket, some T-shirt's and a denim. Though it was a month long trip and my visas were sorted but I wanted to experience the local life.

I didn't wanted to just sightsee and come back, I actually wanted to live like locals and experience their culture and lifestyle firsthand.

I took a train for Mumbai and from there my flight was scheduled late at night, Mumbai to Seoul, Incheon airport on a Qatar Airways airbus A350. The flight was 14 hours long with a layover at Doha for 3 hours.

The opportunity that I got, I don't think everyone gets that, my compilation of stories was saved as a first draft in my boss's computer, my daughter was taken better care than me and I was travelling to my dream destination for a month. You can look at half empty glass or the half filled one; its your choice to look at life. Everything was fine except the fact that he would be sitting next to me on this plane holding my hand just like he did on our honeymoon.

His letter was in my wallet, it always accompanied me no matter where I go. Instead of weakness I made it my strength.

Every time I faced a difficult situation, I opened it and like magic some lines of the letter would make sense to me and I would come out of that situation with a solution in my hand.

After landing at Incheon, the first thing I did was getting a local SIM card to call back home and inform that I have reached safely and then I changed my currency from INR to Korean Won. 1 INR is 15 WON. Korea is not that expensive to live if you choose to travel by express trains and busses, eat at local street vendors rather than big restaurants and live in a hostel instead of a hotel.

I carefully planned all my travel; bus and train passes, took maps and tourist brochures to get my knowledge and language was no barrier to me owing to years of watching Korean dramas, I knew the basic Korean language.

I had pre planned my stay, for the first fifteen days I had booked a hostel in Hongdae and the second half in Itaewon. Both the surroundings were good for students, first time visitors, short or long term expats.

I might have to write another book to tell you about my raw experiences in Seoul. The Korean food is so lip smacking, one should definitely try out kimchi, bibimbap, japchae, ddukbokki. I made so many friends at the hostel, got connected with foreigners who were travelling solo.

I covered each and every bit on my camera and simultaneously on my diary, I went on late night walks on the Hannam beach, the Hannam bridge was so mesmerising to look at in the night. I wished Nick could see all this through me. Had be been here; I would have irritated him by calling oppa oppa, we would have got drunk on soju and then he would have carried me on his back to make insane love to me. My eyes got watery.

One day I was travelling to Jeju island, I was on a train after which I had to take a ferry to reach there. I got a text from Sunita Ma'am, "call asap, urgent." She was infamous for sending strictly short and work related texts.

I called on her WhatsApp number, she picked up instantly, "listen to this, it's a big news for you, I sent your manuscript to some big publishing houses and pinch yourself, your work is selected by the best, 'Ink 9 Publishers' and they are keen in publishing it right away."

"Are you serious Ma'am, I can't believe this," I covered my mouth in sheer euphoria.

"Yes yes very much serious, even I couldn't believe my ears when their chief editor called me quoting that it was the perfect book for that quarter of the year and it had that X factor of becoming a bestseller."

"I don't even have words to thank you ma'am"

"You have put enough words to write a bestselling book, but there is one problem." She seemed calm for saying a problem.

"What problem?"

"You completed the book but where's the title? Did you forget to give your book a name or is it purposely left for us to give you suggestions?"

"I don't know Ma'am, I just didn't have anything in my mind with which this book should be published." I looked outside the window.

"But the publishers want a title and that too asap, they have already started designing cover pages and I will mail you the options."

"Tell me what title you want to give, haven't you thought of something specific?"

I could see the sea nearing, the ripples in the water were matching the ripples created in my mind. The view outside was so scenic just like a day dream, for a flash of second I saw Nick smiling and waving out to me from the end of the port.

I saw him wearing his uniform and the Maroon Beret. He was nodding his head as if affirming that I did the right thing. He was happy wherever he was, his eyes were twinkling with love, his hand gestures were asking me about Anna. I heard him calling out to me, "Mrs captain, I love you."

Sunita Ma'am's voice brought me back, "Aisha, can you hear me? Give me a title."

"Mrs captain" I closed my eyes and reassured myself with a broad smile.

"Sorry?"

I shouted out loud letter by letter, "***MRS CAPTAIN***."